Mary Fides Shepperson

Harp of Milan

Mary Fides Shepperson

Harp of Milan

ISBN/EAN: 9783337429652

Printed in Europe, USA, Canada, Australia, Japan

Cover: Foto ©Andreas Hilbeck / pixelio.de

More available books at **www.hansebooks.com**

SHEPPERSON,

1897.

J. H. YEWDALE & SONS CO.,

MILWAUKEE, WIS.

PREFACE.

The great Aeolian Harp of Milan extended from the house of Harold El Zagel to the rear of the Church of St. Ambrose. The Milanese record that this Harp preserved, and at times reproduced, the dominant passions that had burnt beneath it.

Harold El Zagel tells us that his house was thronged nightly with people striving to hear this voice of the spirit. He also relates that "the night following the wedding of Count Chialfoz and his fair bride—while yet the city was re-echoing the voices of song, laughter, congratulation—the Harp took up the spirit of joy. The sound thereof was the vocal exponent of happy thoughts, hopes, tender longings, desires, untried loves, Heaven-born aspirations, that lay voiceless in the crowd below. The listening city became still as the stars. It was sweet—that voice of hope which had been nourished in silence so long; it was tender as the smile of the Blessed—that love which had watched o'er the graves of the years; it was strong with the strength of eternity—that promise of the soul's true home."

"As though," Harold El Zagel continues, "the bells of midnight had power to annihilate time and to arouse the Spirit of the Past, oft-times in re-echo of these bells, forgotten heart throbs rushed forth from out the silence encircling Space and Time, and vibrated in mystic melody through the Harp. A midnight melody of great beauty and pathos is called by the people the "Death Scene of St. Ambrose."

"Sweeter music never left its Heaven. Mingled with the breath of pain, which ceased only with the music, all worthy feelings of life sang as it were of triumph. A low minor of great sweetness was called the "Kindness of St. Ambrose;" another chord more breath-like in which the alto Pain predominated, was called his "Friendship for Augustine;" a strain of spirit-like joy was named the "Baptism of Augustine." But above the strain and the triumph arose the song of Peace. Peace modulated into holiness while Silence adored—silent the Alps now—silent the river, the city, the stars. O Silence! Child of Eternity! the depths of Thought are thine, the hearts of men, the white lips of the dead, the lowest waters of ocean, the space homes of the stars. Linger yet, while, from the death-bed guarded by holiness, Heaven shall call the soul. Sweet as anthems of angels, faint as the breath of the dying, chaste as the Alpine couch of purity and peace, kind as the night-winds of Calvary rose—sank—trembled—ceased the "Call of Heaven."

We have given paraphrases of the Harp Songs as found in Harold El Zagel's manuscripts. Of this person we have only such desultory knowledge as may be gleaned from scattered fragments of manuscripts found among the Harp Songs. From them we learn that he was of Spanish-English origin; a wanderer, probably an invalid, residing with his mother in Milan. A spirit of gloom pervades his writings except when influenced by his mother whom we may conclude to have been a woman of education, talent, and piety. In the following extract, he, speaking of his mother, says: "Out from the long buried Past came her story. How the fair English girl of the Convent School in Italy was about to consecrate her life to God; pure passionless life, uneventful as the life of flowers in the Convent garden. How the happy days of school life closed; the graduates' Cross glittered on her neck; the kind farewells were spoken,—just for one month, one little month, in which to visit England, to receive her father's blessing, to kneel by the grave of the mother whom she had never known, and then,—to return, to die to the world, to live for God. Ah! month replete with destiny! For Harold Hastings, ever restless, ever enterprising, welcomed to his halls the Spanish enthusiast, the inventor of the diving-bell,—Giovanni El Zagel. Ah, Alice Hastings! the trees are murmuring 'round your Convent home, murmuring of change, of sorrow; but you hear them not. The faces of saints in the Convent Chapel are sad to-night, but you see them not. The memories of conscience are calling,—calling like the bell that is ringing for prayers for the dead in the Convent chapel so far away, but you hear them not.

Who shall blame the young heart in its first fond

dream, or who shall know that the bride of earth was meant to be the bride of Heaven?

Six happy months passed by replete with pleasure and love. Giovanni El Zagel and his wife, weary of travel, took up their abode in the courtly cottage nestling amid the blue hills of Teheran.

A new experiment, child of the restless brain, called Giovanni from his happy home to tempt once more the gloomy grandeur of the water world. The yellow waters of the Persian Gulf kept well their secret. Perhaps they did not care that the dark comely head and passionate heart should soon be still low in the home of pearls. Surely the sunlight laughed,—laughed in the high blue sky, laughed o'er the cottage watching from the hill, laughed o'er the cheerful words, the light good by, laughed o'er—his grave.

My father whom I never knew! Dark eyes that never met my own save from the gilded frame upon my nursery wall! Heir am I of his doubting mind, his ever restless heart; heir of my mother's sorrow."

Again speaking of some sorrow which had come upon him, he says: "I could not rise above my fate. Blue rose the undulating hills of Teheran, clear was the sky above, peaceful the white head stones of the dead. All nature breathed indifference, tranquility,—a life serene, not consonant, not ours. I turned from nature to the quiet of my room. The pictures upon the wall gleamed with a human sympathy. I shuddered with Beatrice Cenci at the Mannaia. O Earth! your sad, sad woe rolls on; and we, drifting upon its tide, claim kindred with a sorrow that is still—A low rustle, a light footstep, and my mother's hand rested upon my arm."

Among the songs of ten years' later date we find the following: "O that a hand might come from out the storm, the darkness, the despair! O that a voice might speak, till one by one these phantoms pass away; till back they hasten, back to their hell, —these hideous doubts and fears! 'If life were all, my child, I would weep with you. If this poor mound of earth were all that remains of the human heart which has lived and loved and suffered, I would weep with you. The song of earth is a song of woe; the life that ends with the grave is a distorted thing; the poet heart which wanders not beyond the narrow things of time must—break'."

This is all that can be gathered of the personal history of Harold El Zagel.

Knowing how much expression and even thoughts suffer in translation, we have no hope that the songs here published shall, even in a remote way, resemble the subtle music of the Harp. The pristine force is gone, many connecting melodies are lost; and, without the prose introductions which shall in a measure convey the subject matter, the songs themselves are become almost unintelligible.

THE AUTHOR.

SOUNDS OF RESTLESSNESS AND SOUNDS OF SORROW.

Crying still as they cried of old,—the Harpies of the legend, the Sirens of the song; the lament of Jeremiah, the groan of Gautama,—yea, down thro' the ages, in the songs of Byron, the "Sorrows of Werther,"—desire, unrest, afflictions of the soul.

Where shall the surges of the soul waves cease?
Thro' all the world I wander seeking peace.

It was night; and through the great Aeolian Harp of the world arose sounds of restlessness and sounds of sorrow. Spain lamented her children. With the sob of wife and children mingled the death groan on the Cuban battle-field. The warm breath through the Harp was the burning village of Guira Melena. The measured sound was the march to battle, and the steel-music of midnight was the clash of machete and sabre.

With a voice of the conquered cities of Alexander and of Caesar, with the cry of the burning Capitol of Carthage, Armenia lay prostrate, lamenting.

Cold as the Alpine dawn, salt as tears of the night, came a breath from the sea. Frost bands held not the vessel, storms were with Aeolus; only the sighs of earth's sleepers had lingered in mist o'er the ocean,—but the "Elbe" was sinking.

Sounds from awakening cities! Surely the Angel of Dawn weeps o'er the sorrows that awaken at her coming! Sleep had brought rest to the laborer, dreams to the sad heart, forgetfulness to eyes that are watching, to hearts that are waiting; silence and peace had blessed all. But, alas! what sights await the dawn! O sad Rhine river, Loire, and Thames, from out your tides some Harriet Shelley's face stares at the dawn! In the palace, in the home, in the hovel, Death has been; and they lie equal now, —the weary Czar of Russia, the mother of the home, the wretched babe of Regent Street. And there are sadder sights. O Angel of Dawn, lament! Lament the victims of Toil, the wrecks of Passion, the cries of Rachel for her children, of David for Absalom; the weariness of old age, the white grave-stones rising from hearts; the hopes which await the vessel that lies beneath the storm; the maniac and his Hell, the murderer, the suicide, the condemned cell,—the scaffold. Ah! it was morn; and through the great Aeolian Harp of the world arose sounds of restlessness and sounds of sorrow.

HARP ECHOES.

THE POET-PHILOSOPHER.

I.

He stood alone amid thousands: too cognizant of sorrow to be selfish; too great for a thought of bitterness against the pitiful hands that struck him.

Life as a falling star, rose—sank in eternity and the poet-philosopher waited and watched. With the eye of a Gibbon he walked midst the Middle Ages; with the heart of the Wandering Jew he gazed on the history of nations; with the kind human heart of Gautama he pitied the frailties of mortals. Had he himself essayed the higher Path? the path of purity, universal charity, self-denial? Had he become strong and holy victor in the Lerna strife? Glorious is the height of virtue whence the eyes unawed survey Time and Eternity. There only we stand in the shadow of God's peace; there have our noble hearts advanced into the light of God's peace; there have our martyrs and saints died inebriated with God's peace. Had the heart of the hero become less vigilant because the giant warriors, Passion and Pride, were wounded and the sounds of battle were low? Had he fallen from virtue's height? O woe! there's a gash in the soul which the years shall not heal. Well if the great lesson shall be learned at last,—that we are most truly God-like when most kindly human; well if, extending the hand of beneficent kindness to the creatures of our London Strand, our Broadways, our Madeleine boulevards, our work houses, jails, penitentiaries, we may exclaim with the God-man, "Neither do I condemn you;" well if that great scar on the soul shall interpret for him the history of ages, the troubled panorama of to-day, the humiliating atonement of death, the tragedy of Calvary, the Credo of the Church, the peace waiting home of the soul.

II.

He stood mid the wintry stillness of a Canadian forest. The scene was magically weirdly beautiful: the snows as frozen coldnesses enveloped the trees;

the zenith moon, the stars shone cold as resenting the weary monotony of their mystery; the broad, white snow world waited and scorned not and hoped not.

His heart was the wintry stillness of a Canadian forest. Out from his life had sunk the youth-constellations. Then he had cried aloud, but Pride stood beside him and pointed to other men's lives and showed him the thing in the semblance. In the politic smile lay the sneer, in the lip laugh the eyes' scorning, and the flowers of compliment, friendship, and love were set in heart shading. Over white graves in hearts the snows were ceaselessly falling and men laughed and forgot. There lay an early love, there lay enthusiasm, there lay wide trust in another, and by it lay human kindness. So he walked forth with Pride.

III.

Ever the atmosphere rises and revels in unrest. Her million animalcules have lives commensurate with their motion and rest for them means death. In the elemental world liveth and reigneth unrest. In the rock, gigantic, o'erfrowning the deep, change is enacting. At its base the water ocean entices the elements from their compounds, at its summit the air-ocean entices the elements from their compounds and there is struggle, disintegration, transmutation—then on the victors go exulting in the strong joy of affinity, unrest,—change. Aye, on the victors go to meet that which shall call, with a yet stronger voice, to atoms of their molecules, and there shall be struggle, decomposition, unrest,—change. O paradox of the chemic world, where life is death and death transition! O compounds that

4

we break at will and compounds that we form, yet are your elements sacred for they are from eternity! The scientist turned from his laboratory. Worthy at heart he was but proud. The church bells were chiming Adeste for it was Christmas eve. The flames from a tall blast-furnace played grandly on a back-ground of black sky. He called the flames by name "I know you Calcium, Carbon, Silicon—. I know the spectra of your flames. I know what you have been what you shall be—but the life-heat of the flame, the non-annihilation, the brilliance, the wild freedom—whence? whither? With the alchemists of old I have analyzed gold, but I cannot make gold; I have analyzed organic matter, I know the elements of life but I cannot make life; I have analyzed flame, I know—nothing." Mildly the stars looked down as pitying the proud impotence of his soul, and the churches chimed Adeste.

IV.

He stood 'neath the Northern Aurora. How essentially unsympathetic is the physical world with the Ego of each heart! As an Armenian refugee on the London Strand, so is the heart in the universe. Who shall describe thee, O Night of the Northern Aurora! The cold magnetic storm was yet sullenly sobbing. 'Twas the Carnival night of the Colors. Steel blue sported with crimson, green pursued amber; hues of the violet, purple, and red rose into scarlet. Scarlet was mother and queen. Scarlet spread down o'er the snows, o'er the hills, o'er the ice-bergs. Scarlet grew pale in pity for earth and the gay colors triumphed. Yellow and purple contend in an emerald cloud wave; crimson and amber embrace in steel-blue. Quick coruscations—palpitating light—'Twas the Carnival

5

night of the Colors; with Earth it was Lent—earnest and solemn; with the heart 'twas the Eve of the Passion. Out from the Past they came,—the loves that had perished; slow at their side stalked the dreams of the years; Doubt the deriding and scornful led into the shade of the iceberg and thence watched the world. O flame of the heart! burn low, burn down to peace. All whom thou lovest are far from thee; thou hast entered the Northern night in far Franz Josef Land. May the mountain shadows o'er unbroken snows bring thee repose! May the slow solemnity of the glacier, the majestic motion of icebergs, the star bound quiet of the abode of the vast, the awful, the sublime—bring thee repose. And far away in the Christian land the churches chimed Adeste.

V.

He was kind, and his kindness had no return, therefore he perished.

With honest earnest eyes he had watched life, unawed by the gloom hanging over its origin, frowning over its end. A soul strong in the strength of immortality, joyous in its own kindness; hopeful, confident in the reflex beam of its own probity,—such a soul had blessed the world, had made the world better because he lived. But the bright head is low to-night, the weary face asks "Do not wake me."

He was kind and his kindness had no return, therefore he perished.

Why should the world be gay when people are
    moaning and dying;
  What is the glory of earth unto a spirit of pain?
Why should the wheel revolve after the main belt
    is broken?
  Why should the sister-stars call sisters that come
    not again?

Now I remember a voice that spoke to the noble
    within me,
  Out of the silence it came—glorious, possible
    thing;
Why did it fade because I smiled to the greeting
    of Caesar?
  Why does it wait in my grave—Angel of ebony
    wing?

Cold is the mountain of mist, but colder the sun
    without Caesar,
  Glorious god of the world, great in the gloom of
    the grave.
Yet does it rise in my soul—O Protean sorrow of
    sorrows!
  Where I have loved I am lost, what I have loved
    will not save.

Over the glittering grief, rises a sorrow that trem-
    bles;
  Far in the mist at my feet, wanders the ebony
    wing.
Why does it bear thro' the gloom the scene of the
    Trial of Jesus?
  Why do I see thee again glorious possible thing?

Why does it wait in my grave—the scene of the
    Trial of Jesus?
If I consent I believe, if I believe I despair.
Why does my soul grasp the light that fades in the
    greeting of Caesar?
Black! black! black! is my soul as the grave of
    pines calling me there.

THE CENTENARIANS.

We are very, very old!
Each to-morrow is a dreary yesterday;
We are waiting, waiting, waiting, for the call which
    shall summon us away
        Out of the world.

For the children have become us—and they say
The self same things we said;
They smile upon each other with the eyes that smile
    upon us from the holy dead,
        Beyond the world.

If, Tithonus-like, we cannot die
Of all mortals, are we most unblest.
Peace o'er the white hearse passing! Little one
    soon hast thou found that which the old heart
    longs for—rest
        Beyond the world.

Peace o'er the white mounds gleaming on the hill,
Strange peace within the heart!
God's angels call us and their breath is cold.
Press down the eyelids—we are very old, and we
    depart
        Out of the world.

THE GANGES.

Roll, mighty Ganges! roll, thou lordly tide!
   A thousand summers greet thine effluent wave,
A thousand blessings on thy course abide,
   Yet is thy source cold in its glacial grave.

The gay hall glitters and the music wakes,
   The dancers grow embodied melody;
The snow of flowers descends in pearly flakes,
   'Tis sunlight on the Ganges near the sea.

They place the crown on the dead poet's brow,
   They title him the "lost Divinity;"
They wreathe his bier with many roses now,—
   'Tis sunlight on the Ganges near the sea.

The source!—ah! back, back in a glacial grave,
   Solemn and stern and dark and very cold.
Whence springs the Ganges, while her effluent wave
   Sparkles in sunshine girt by sands of gold.

SAFE FOREVER.

Safe forever, little one,
   But my heart is aching;
Where the human currents run,
   Human hopes are breaking.

Rest forever, little one,
   Past the sounds of sorrow;
While the weary wander on,
   Down the vast to-morrow.

9

Peace forever, little one,
  Past the troubled waking;
Yet where human currents run,
  Human hopes are breaking.

WANDERER.

Art thou dreaming, tender hearted,
  Of the restless ones who roam?
Have the children all departed
  From thy heart and home?

AGED PARENTS.

There are life affections broken,
  Lying painless 'neath the sod;—
There are names that are not spoken
  Save between the soul and God.

There were childish hearts that missed us,
  Ere the life storm left us old;
There were childish lips that kissed us,
  Which are loveless now and cold.

There is error, there is sorrow,
  There is restlessness and pain;
Yet the heart cries to each morrow
  "Bring the children back again!"

THE DYING ARAB.

All of earth is drear to me,
      Arabíe;
Lone I lie and dream of thee,
      Arabíe:

Now I drink the fragrant breeze
'Neath the pure Pimento trees;—
Now I hear the roaring seas.
    ·   Arabíe.

All my spirit cries aloud,
    Arabíe,
O'er the world in foamy shroud
    Arabíe;
While each mile of land and wave
Seems to hold some life hope's grave
O'er whose gloom the surges rave.
    Arabíe.

I am in a foreign land,
    Arabíe,
And I cannot understand,
    Arabíe;
While the many pass me by,
Heeding not my starving cry,
And I lay me down to die.
    Arabíe.

Oh! from out the sunny land,
    Arabíe!
But to touch one kindred hand,
    Arabíe;
But to hear the liquid flow
Of the language that we know.
But to hear and answer low.
    Arabíe.

I am sinking unto death,
    Arabíe.
Now I drink the flower breath.
    Arabíe;
'Tis the allspice on the breeze,
'Neath the white Pimento trees,
And the realm of dreamless ease,
    Arabíe.

THE ALPS.

Glorious sunset o'er the mountains!
    Mighty pillars of the cloud,
Crimson sullen plains of heaven,
    Gild yon glacier cold and proud;
    Like our love world in a shroud.

Fades yon bird within the glowing
    Of a crimson incense-bond.
Hark! the bugles chilly blowing
    From the glacial gloom beyond.

Isolated scenes of nature,
    Cold and high, uncomplemented;
Lone in pain and lone in grandeur,
    I dwell here contented.

Far beyond the clouds of sunset,
    Soars my soul to sink in Thee;—
That of which I am an atom,
    God—and God's eternity.

THE MISSIONARY.

And thou art dead! Brave, generous heart, rest on!
    Thy noble sorrows consecrate thy tomb.
Our martyred one, God's smile is over thee
    Gilding the darkness of thine early doom.
Beauty and holiness, angels await to bless,—
    Loved, lost, deplored!
Slumber now peacefully, loved by that Deity
    Our souls adored.

Ah! I hear the north wind calling thro' the pines,
And I hear the gentle rain drops on the vines,
  And I see the home forests wave;
But I waken at the Orinoco's mouth,
'Neath the burning waves of light in the South,
  Alone by his grave.

Our martyred one, from that bright home above,
  Look on thy brother-soul in sorrow here:
Plead my petition at God's throne of love,
  That he may give me grace to persevere.
For all of light closes in rayless night;
  No phosphorescent glitter on life's wave.
Last of our band, lone in this burning land,
  Dying beside his grave.

Ah! I hear the holy Office pealing forth,
From our Monastery chapel in the North,
  Where the pine forests wave;
But I waken at the Orinoco's mouth,
'Neath the burning waves of light in the South
  Alone by his grave.

DISSONANCE.

Far have I wandered from Thee,
  My Father, the mountain is cold;
I would turn from the mist and the mad mystery.
  I would kneel in the fold.

For we cannot understand,
  And the days evolve our fate,
While the night with starry hand
  Writes the warning—"wait!"

Wait secure in the humble fold,
  Wait, the longing of soul shall cease;
Wait till the fiat of God is told,
  Wait and there shall be peace.

My God, I would come back to Thee,
  Too God-like art Thou to repel;
'Tis the spark of Thyself that Thou gavest to me
  Which seeking its high flame—fell.

Wounded and willing to wait,
  Willing to trust for the best;
Willing to bend by the sunset gate
  Which borders the land of rest.

Weary of all that is low,
  Astray in the misty unknown:
Too cold in the mists of the mountain of snow
  Too far o'er the crowd and too lone.

The lights of the valley shine warm,
  The gray spire reposes with men:
Shall I stand on the height and complain of the
      storm?—
  I will enter the valley again.

Enter the valley and enter the church,
  Enter the dim confessional,
The soul storm shall cease, the heart shall find
      peace,
  And God's absolution shall fall over all.

THE AVALANCHE.

Behold the snow bound city,
 The fair-haired bride of night!
But little Nellice moans in pain,
 The proud frost spirits laugh again,
And thro' the icy air
 A voice in prayer:—
"Above the world in white,
 In a home warm and bright;
Oh! let the spirit wander in a world of starry light."

'Tis an angel of the snow,
 Breathing o'er me freezing breath;
But my duty points to Blanche
 'Neath the cruel avalanche,
And I sink in snowy shroud,
 And I breathe in cirrus cloud;
Oh! the crimson life-tide flows
 Tingeing all the silent snows;
Closer now the frozen breath,
 And I sink in waiting death.

Oh! the broken hearts to-night,
 Oh! the mighty avalanche,
 Little Blanche!
How yon glacier shone this morn,
 And majestic Matterhorn!
Ere to-morrow's sun shall rise
 The eternal meets our eyes,"—
Faster now the crimson tide
 "Jesu, mercy" Nellice cried
And she died.

O'er the dead in snowy bed
 Burst the morning sun;
And the wailing lamentation,
 Universal desolation

Gilded by the pale red ray,
  Seemed the dawn of that great day,
When the span of life is run,
  And the world is done.

STORM.

Our Father, there are storms upon the deep,
  And human souls are crying helplessly;
Lost human souls night's waiting watches keep,
  With frozen gaze fixed on Eternity.
O the strong and mighty waters!
  O the world of moving waves!
The moon shining full, and the lone sea gull
  Guarding our graves.

Our Father, there are storms upon life's sea,
  They rage around us and obscure our goal;
Oh! let one ray of light glimmer to-night,
  For icy pain is gathering o'er the soul.
O the strong o'er mastering sorrow!
  O the pain that may not cease!
Twilight memories thronging, o'er the soul's rest-
      less longing,
  And we cry,—"peace, peace!"

POETS' GRAVES.

  Where Keats and Shelley sleep,
    The poet heart must sigh;
  Must with Religion weep,
    And then pass by.

  Must pause with solemn heart,
    In Hucknall's old church yard;
  Where lies the mortal part
    Of love and sorrow's bard.

16

Lord Byron, o'er thy grave
The long gray grasses wave,
And thou hast slumbered long,
O restless child of song!

OLD DUTIES.

Old duties, welcome! So you're back again,
    And ye are ladened as the autumn sheaves.
What! is there languor in the extended hand?
    It must not be. Life is an earnest thing,
Strong, neutral background whereon Heaven shall
        paint
Eternity with colors of to-day.
Welcome, our duties! Stand across the years,
    Unfold each day; and wrap each solemn night
In thy approving smile. And life shall be
    Calm in the strength that suffers and endures;
Patient and prayerful 'mid the hosts of wrong;
    Divinely human where the ignoble err.
So shall the soul be happy in its God,
    When Duty signs the cross above our graves.

PROMISES.

Unreal, unreal;—
    As falls the petal from the rose,
        As drift the leaves in autumn wind,
    As summer glories under winter snows,
        So are they fallen,—
                Life's promises.

Unreal, unreal;—
    O restless human heart!
        The mirage yet recedes as we appear,
    Ah! 'tis the glow of hope loth to depart;
        So are they fleeing,—
                Life's promises.

17

Unreal, unreal;—
Where is that land of rest?
Where shall the surges of the soul waves
cease?
Where is that all we crave of purest, holiest,
best?
O Saviour of the world! where is thy peace?
"In Heaven."

DRINK, BUT YE SHALL THIRST AGAIN.

'Twas a scene of magic beauty in a forest of the
West,
For the toil of day had ended and all nature
breathed of rest;
E'en the long grass, e'en the laurels, e'en the trees
did peaceful wave:
Mellow skies, suffused in crimson, watched the
sun's all glowing grave
Rose the home fires, came the dear ones, while all
earthly longings cease
Came the benison from Heaven, came the words
of peace.
And the human heart was happy, while I heard a
sad refrain;
"Drink, but ye shall thirst again."

Thou art crowned, our angel beauty! Alice, thou
art crowned to-day;
O'er the bold eye, o'er the bright eye, fair haired
blue eyed Queen of May.
Little Alice, little Alice, night is weaving shreds
with day;
Little Alice, little Alice, roses fade away.
And the human heart was happy, while I heard a
sad refrain;
"Drink, but ye shall thirst again."

SORROW.

Afar the sounds of earthly sorrows roll.
   Ah! in our misery,
   Whet a nonentity,
   All human things may be.
While anguish rages in the inmost soul.
   Oh! how we bend in woe,
Where the heart bleedeth;
   Though all the world below
Our solace needeth;
   Tho' storms of passion blow,
Tho' tears of sorrow flow,
   Yet lone we bend in woe,
When the heart bleedeth.

None was so brave as he—our fallen one,
   None was so fair as she—our child that died;
None know as we must know
   Our own peculiar woe,
Our joy, our hope, our pride.
   Let the dead lie softly sleeping,
Let the living heart arise;
   Grandly, thro' the night of sorrow,
Let us paint beyond the skies
   Scenes of love for weeping eyes.

All is common; and our soul-cry is but part
   Of a universal lamentation;
And that white head-stone gleaming on our
     heart
   Marks one of common graves
Vast as the foam of waves
   O'er deluged desolation.

THE SIMOOM.

Sultry was the desert air,
　And the cloudless sky was fair;
Deep the sunbeam burned the sand,
　Winds of fire waved o'er the land,
Hot exhaustion pressed our band.

Cease, O Sun! thine every beam
　Is a heavy burning stream.
Cease, and sink within thy West;
　Madly is thy power confessed,
Cease to burn us,—let us rest!

Hell comes on in heat and gloom,
　And we see the wild simoom;
Black and broad the fiend draws nigh,
　By our camels low we lie,
Waiting but the power to die.

Fear and might have worked their will,
　And the broken mind is still.
Rolls the tumult, whirls the sand,
　Dying eyes on native land
Gaze; and peace is over all.

　Hear the heavenly rain-drops fall!
Falls the evening cool and still
　As he quaffs the endless rill:
Gentle fingers lave his brow,
　Loving voices murmur now
As his lips are pressed
　"Thou art weary, rest!"

Rise we to the sandy main;
　He will never rise again.
Ah! thy mother should have pressed
　Thy young head upon her breast,
Tears and prayers should soothe thy rest.

Turn and leave the fair-haired child,
　Ah! his parting hour was wild
Yet it seems in death he smiled.

ELAINE.

"Truly our world is fair," she said,
　"The love-birds thrill the air,
The clouds are veiled in lace pale-red
　The breeze holds fragrance rare
The waving trees rich beauty shed."
　She said, "the world is fair."

She said, "Ye glowing happiness,
　Ye love-bird minstrelsy,
Ye are without the power to bless
　The child of misery;
And mid ye I am comfortless."
　She said, "O pity me!"

"For memories come of dreams that were
　All happy and all kind,
And hopes that painted empty air
　With longings of the mind."
She said, "they left with promise fair
　And sorrow stayed behind."

CHANGE.

O ancient world! thy ruins round me lie;
　Ye speak in words of peace unto my soul.
All that has been beneath yon sullen sky,
　All that now is from ice-bound pole to pole,
All that shall be while Sol's great car shall roll,
　Form but their parts in Time's capacious whole.

Here Dardenelles becomes the Hellesponte.
　Abydos seeks her youth and beauty—where?

The night is darkening over Sestos' hills,
  And Hero smiles, verging a life's despair.

Troy stands again surrounded by her foes,
  And Helen gazes with a spirit moved.
Achilles raves about the funeral pyre
  Of him—his friend,—Patroclus, the beloved.

Ah! Babylon, proud Paris of the Past!
  Thy chariots dash along thy mighty wall.
Thy thousand towers smile o'er thy flowery domes,
  And Baal, poor idol, recks not of thy fall.

O God! above, beyond the sullen skies;
  God knowing all, from cause to final close;
Under thy guidance take thy weary child,
  And in that quiet let my soul repose.

TEMPTATION.

All day the long grief surges o'er the soul.
  Thrice welcome, Night! the iron guard may fall.
And gentlest sleep enfolds the wounded thing
  Which bleeding cries "my duty, and my all."

All day upon the soul's high battle ground
  The passions fight against the lordly will.
Pale victor, there is truce across the world
  And night o'er sobbing day cries, "peace, be
    still!"

O God! the hidden strife is hard to bear.
  The mailed morrow follows down the West.
And waits the awakening of a weary world;
  And only in the grave my heart shall rest.

The long, long conflict, and the frequent fall.
  Dark laid mosaic of unknown design;
With lights of mercy, shades of penitence,
  What may ye yet be in a plan divine?

RESURGAM.

I have stood over the ruins of Palmyra and of Babylon; I have asked for the things that have been, but no answer came from the silence. I have bent with the madman, Hugh Miller, over earth's history written in the rocks; I have beheld, in the stratified cliff, the sun-work of a million years. I have seen the formations of different aeons cemented into one rock, and have traced the story of upheavals and gigantic perturbations. Yea, I have watched wide ocean breaking into spray, bursting her thousand bonds, leaping unto the stars, falling into the continents;—while from her central stillness Alps have risen. And I have questioned the rocks: "What of the Past?" But no answer came from the silence.

I have stood in Greenwood, in Pere-la-Chaise, in Westminster. How peaceful are these abiding places of the dead! With the voice of prophecy they speak, but, Cassandra like, they are unheeded. The forms that once held talent, beauty, genius lie at my feet; but talent, beauty, genius—where are they? Thales of Miletus might answer: "Nothing is produced, nothing is destroyed; the Protean elements live through transition and clothe themselves in appearances." The unanalyzed Motive Cause, with its unanswered How and Why, rises from Thales' philosophy, waits over Pere-la-Chaise, over the world. Reason has failed. The grave of the new born babe holds its secret secure 'neath her search lights. Reason admits that she has failed. Poor finite wanderer, wandering amidst the thoughts of God! Let us call her home! Let her be only the noblest offspring of Time, nay better let her wed strong Faith, the Child of Eternity.

Holding the Creed of the Church I have stood in Greenwood, in Pere-la-Chaise, in Westminster, and I have said to Brooklyn, Paris, London: "When Change and Time shall have been; when all the rosy sleepers of to-night shall lie in beds more narrow; when the great life-tide round the world to-night shall have rolled, Protean, down the ages; when the splendid pageant—theaters, palaces, courts, thrones, House of Parliament, Notre Dame and the proud record of mighty names, national honors, noble battle-fields, shall have become chapters in Ancient History;—nay when Brooklyn, Paris, London, shall have become Palmyras of the Past, even then shall my soul be young.

I have bowed low in reverent wonder 'neath the stars of winter midnight. With pain of soul I have regarded them in the fancy light of Science,—so far that they seem near, so rapid that they seem stationary! Weary is the paradox! In utter absence of meaning rise the figured lines of space.

With pride of soul I have regarded the stars as the creatures of my Creator. On the mild glory of Night have I gazed and claimed kinship with the farthest star. In the still order of our Solar System, in the majestic motion, emanative of the Primum Mobile, strongly controlling universes, have I recognized the intelligence of that Being who created me. Nay, holding the Creed of the Church I have said to the stars, "Glorious art thou, Arcturus, Sirius, Procyon! In frost-mist splendor, confused glory, ye are fair—Suns of the galaxy! Yet when aeons shall have passed away; when suns, systems, universes shall have burned out, and from their smouldering ashes shall have arisen the Phoenix glory of a new heaven—even then shall my soul be young.

I have stood 'neath the Northern Aurora. Surely the artist of the firmament had wrought magnificently that inverted cloud fountain of light. A hand from the space world reaching to the zenith heavens beckoned to the Colors. Warm, humble, happy, they assembled 'neath the hand that caressed them, then their blessedness diffusing extended in widening streamers and rested broadly upon the horizon; then their blessedness suffusing broke, commingled, changed; became warmth, shadows, smiles, hues, shades, tints,—the glorious color world. Surely the artist of earth had wrought magnificently the North's snow-garment. Perfectly fitting it lay over the peak of Altus, over the sentinel icebergs, over snow-bound ocean and earth. Holding the Creed of the Church I have said to the Northern Aurora, "Thou art a creature of my Creator; let us praise Him! And kneeling in contemplation of that primal Being of whom all beauty is an effluence I have adored.

I have trodden earth's battle fields. Yet where shall the foot of man rest and stand not upon them; Marathon, Cannae, Pharsalia, Waterloo, the way of Alexander, the retreat from Moscow, the cities of Carthage and of Rome,—these are earth's battlefields, earth's cemeteries. Not where the headstones glitter, there lie the sleepers of to-day, but in the heart of our cities, in the deep stillness of our seas, yea constituent of the earth itself lie the sleepers of the ages.

There is a mythical story which says that in the decomposition and transition of each human body, one atom, or molecule, untransmutable, indestructible remains: that this germ is to the future body what the acorn is to the oak; that quintillions of such molecules form the dust beneath our feet; and that the favored few who have secured the favor of the Spirit of the Resurrection may hear, upon applying the atomed particle to the ear when overshadowed by the angel's wing, the word Resurgam.

With a smile at the beautiful thought, with a heart
oppressed by the spirit of Time, of Mystery, of
Silence,—yet holding the Creed of the Church I
have said to the sleepers of the ages, "Resurgitis.
Ye live to-day, and ye shall live forever." Forever!
It is a little word but too great for the finite mind.
Is it measurable by numbers? Not by all the numbers in the mind of Pythagoras. By comparison?
Comparisons are of the known, and of time; forever
is of the unknown, and of eternity. By the imag-
ination of Genius? Plato has failed. Even as the
ocean monsters cannot contain the ocean neither
can human minds contain the word "forever." It
encircles us, it encircles the sleepers of the ages.
It extends to every horizon, it rises from every
horizon and glimmers in the zodiac, it wanders
among the stars, it touches God.

HARP ECHOES.

"Physician, heal thyself!" and I reply,
    "The worm of Pain is gnawing at my life
While I rebellious, helpless, must endure.
    'Tis hard to bear this lingering slave of death.
Whose banquet is life-tissue, whose repose
    Is deep within the vaults of human pain;
Who bears secure commission signed by fate
    And whose great shadow falls across the world.
Drugs, opiates, a finished laboratory!
    A hundred painless hasty slaves of death
Would lay me at His feet who sends for me.
    Come, Acids! Monarchs of the chemic-world!
Arsenious, prussic, phosphoric, sulphuric,—
    Short bridge of death! Anticipated fate!
Yet though I hold you, though I love you too
    Strong, latent powers, immortal as myself;

I will not use my will superior
    To call your power against your God and mine.
But come, kind opiates, and friend to man,
    Control this pain, this lingering slave of death,
Let me lie low awhile, nor feel its fang,
    Nor see that shadow looming o'er the world.
Repose is sweet, surcease of pain is peace
    Rest, waveless rest beneath a stormy sea.

II

A voice awoke me in the far off roar,
    A voice reproving yet divinely kind.
"The world rolls on, earth-child, nor will it pause
    At thy sad cry, nor yet if thou wert dead
Would one vibration of its iron heart
    Thrill o'er the tide because thou art no more.
Because the world is selfish, I am loth
    To speak too harshly of the human heart
Which deifies its sorrow and would claim
    From hearts as selfish and as sorrowful
Consideration, tribute-sympathy.
    One cry mid cries whose echoes rival space:
One waiting death, 'mid deaths commensurate
    With each pulsation of the heart of time.
Poor earth child, sister-soul in bonds of clay!
    Could I but bear thee o'er yon sunset bars,—
"O Spirit," said I weeping, "bear me hence!"
    "I may not now," she answered, for thy soul
Is earth bound in its selfish misery;
    But I will speak to thee of things above,
And I will show thee mysteries below.
    Beyond those western curtains lies a world
Of most resplendent beauty. 'Tis the home
    Of thy companion sisters of the soul,
There is thy rest, thy bliss, thy Heaven, thy God.
    Life is a blessing, child, the curse of life
Is ignorance of this, its destiny.
    While ages o'er the cyclic ages roll,

Eternal as its source, life, glorious life
   Shall thrill through space,—a blessing just to be.
Now I will show thee earthly mysteries,
   And thou shalt hear the "Credo" of the dead.

III.

I woke before Zambezie's lordly falls.
   O grandeur, solitude! I stand alone
Where other human foot has never trod.
   "Nay," said a voice reproving, kind, divine,
"The dead bear witness that they wandered here."
   She raised from off the ground a clod of earth
And smiling on me, placed it in my hand.
   "Child, would'st thou know the mystery here,"
      she said,
"An atom indestructible thou hold'st,
   Unchanged by pressure, force, affinity,
Secure within the acid's fiery breath,
   Secure within Vesuvius' foamy flame,
Secure within the deluge of the world.
   The mighty oak within the kernel lies.
The intrinsic germ of being herein lies,
   With power to attract each wandering element
Unto its primal being, have they roved
   From Patagonia to Spitzbergen's snows.
But hearken, earth-child, tell me what thou hearest."
   And holding close the earth clod to my ear,
I heard a breathing whisper, listening still
   I heard "Resurgam,"—still entranced I stood
Again and yet again "Resurgam" rose.
   The spirit wing withdrawn I heard no more.
O mystic word! the Credo of the dead!
   Resurgam cries the dust beneath our feet.
O mystery o'er life from cause to close!
   O world of life unknown in worlds of life!
My brain grew weary touching the unknown,
   The spirit smile hung o'er me and I sank
Submissive, helpless, 'neath the encircling wing.

Unbroken stillness o'er unbroken snows!
   Horizon to horizon seemed a realm
Where chaste frost spirits watched their loves'
     repose
   And all besides a passive purity.
The smile divine, the spirit at my side
   Embodied snow the wing encircling me,
And lo! the silence is replete with sound.
   Ten thousand crystal snows responsive sing
"Resurgam," one long harmony, again
   "Resurgam" sounds from snows to waiting skies.
"Here many thousand fell," the spirit said,
   "In that ill-fated march Napoleon led
From burning Moscow. In yon frozen tide,
   Three hundred thousand soldiers sank in death
Sad Berizina! it is thence you hear
   The psalm Resurgam, and whereon we tread
Each footstep holds its germ of life to be.
   Again the pain of soul, the pitying wing
The smile divine, unconscious confidence.

V

The hanging gardens bloom in Babylon,
   And flowers vivified in brilliancy
Spring into being and go trilling by.
   Above me in a dome of scarlet light,
An aggregate of roses hill-tops high;
   And living flowers that glide in heavy space
As birds, as fish, as starry brilliancies,
   Gilding the heights of yonder sky-borne ferns.
A tropic forest of the Carbon age:
   A vegetation unfamiliar
The atmosphere not ours, the very form
   Of nature changed and all her elements.
The smile divine, the wing stretched over me;
   Deep darkness, and the voice reproving said,

"We tread the plateau Zoor, beneath the sea,
    And soon I leave thee.   Child, when earth
        restored
Make known unto the world what thou hast heard.
    And thou more nobly bear that nascent life
Whose full fruition fills eternity."
    She ceased to speak, but, silence held the strain
Of voices countless as old ocean's waves.
    "Resurgam" sang the waters, sang the world;
The dead of ocean to the dead of earth
    "Resurgam" sounds the universal cry
Revolving onward to eternity
    Waiting the hush of God across the world.

LIONEL.

We are the sequences whereon evolve
   The full blown evils of another age.

Recorder, here's an item for the world's great fail-
    ure column.
    Write it down to tell the masses, the great masses
      whom we know not,
That the strife which they are striving is tremend-
    ous, is gigantic;
    That with failures life is covered as the forest
      floors of Autumn.
Write it down to tell the masses that a brother lived
    and suffered,
    Suffered long all that they suffer; died in failure,
      yet rejoices.
Does the heart ache? He now painless bowed alone
    in Pain's low prison;
    Wrestled mightily with sorrow, called aloud
      across the darkness.
Is the part a dreary waiting? Oh! life's long and
    weary Waitings!
    Rather tempest, rather battle, rather ten fold con-
    sternation
Rather all the ills of Chaos than the weary helpless
    Waiting.
    Yet our silent brother waited, waited for the
    things that came not.
Are the great affections bleeding? Pitying Christ
    bend kindly o'er us!
    All the world is with the loved one, and the loved
    one has departed.
From the cradle to the cloister, from the cloister
    o'er the wide world,
    Throbbed in love, and throbbed in longing the
    hot poet heart now painless.

Doubts, delusions, disappointments,—all the ills of
  seventy winters
  Fell upon the kindest feelings ever exiled from
  their Heaven.
Let the world pronounce him failure! There is
  glory in the white head,
  Meek and pure and self-enduring that another
  may not suffer;
Scorning to be called a victor in a strife that is
  unworthy.

HARP ECHOES.

By the gentle Guadalquiver lived the dark-eyed
  boy, Lionel.
  Never mother's arms embraced him, friend he
  knew not save old Clothel.
Was she nurse, or aunt, or guardian? Clothel said
  naught, and he knew not.
  This he knew that only Clothel oped the door
  to give him shelter,
Only Clothel met his coming with a smile; and,
  slow removing
  The long pipe, mid fumes of glory told the opium
  dreamer's story.
Told about the gray Alhambra, of the conquest of
  Granada;
  Told the ancient Spanish legends of the Moors
  and captive Christians;
Of the warrior-saint, Gonzales; of the statue of
  Madonna,
  Which descended from the church top when a
  blessed babe was buried;
And again it came in darkness where a mournful
  mother waited,—
  Waited for the love that came not, kissed her into
  breathless slumber.

She herself had seen that statue smile, and lift the
    hand of blessing
  As the children scattered flowers in the Forty
    Hours' procession.
She remembered too the story of the abbess,
    Isabella:
  How she led a life of penance, died the young, the
    long lamented.
How Al Hassan, home returning, lingered long
    where she was buried:
  How a great Italian sculptor wrought in pure
    Carrara marble
Her own image, as in girl-hood, dressed in white
    with long veil flowing,
  As she looked that happy morning when she
    made her First Communion.
Then the statue was erected o'er her grave. O
    marble beauty!
  All the city came to see it, thronged beneath the
    splendid moonlight,
Lingered long amid the tombstones and the quiet
    graves of Sisters,
  Till the holy air resounded with the angelus of
    mid-night.
With the latest sound vibrating, prostrate fell the
    marble beauty.
  There was horror o'er the city. Next day came
    the sad Al Hassan
Said the work had been imperfect, had the statue
    re-erected.
  Yet that night the city slept not; at the angelus
    of mid-night,
Thousands saw the great Madonna slowly turn
    toward the statue,
  Raise the eyes with look reproving. Thousands
    saw the marble beauty

Prostrate fall upon the soft soil—broken in a hundred pieces.
Other legends she remembered, but the dark
eyed boy, Lionel,
Slept beside her on the house top, and the opium
dreamer spoke not.

II

By the gentle Guadalquiver, thus rolled on Lionel's
childhood;
Happy in old Clothel's dream world, happy that
the gentle river
Murmured strains of wondrous promise as he
whistled o'er its waters.
Happy that the stained-glass windows, sixty-two
in the Cathedral,
Told the Creed of Catholic christians, and the
glories of the Blessed;
That the white-cross cemetery, with its vocal
"requiescat,"
Uttered "amen" to the river, to the Church's pic-
tured Credo,
To life's earnest supplications, to the hopes of life's
Hereafter.
Only when the bells of evening, pealing forth from
the Cathedral,
From the Convents, from the churches, chimed in
concert o'er the city,
Came a sense of painful longing, dying far in things
eternal.
Longing for a home, a mother, for a foretaste of
God's promise,
That the unknown shall be made known, that the
asking shall be answered.
More of Heaven than earth was near him as the
Angelus of evening
Sank in crimson beds of sunset watched by sentinel
Sierras.

PART SECOND

O'er the wide world I have wandered, and to-night
    my soul is weary;
  Earth has scenes of wondrous beauty, but my
    soul of soul is weary;
I recall the cloister's quiet while my soul of soul is
    weary.
  Free of heart, a humble brother, dwelt I in the
    monastery;
All the quiet, holy Fathers met me kindly, called
    me Brother,
  And my happy novice-brothers tempered with me
    the bell-metal,
Wrought with me the ponderous church-bells tuned
    the chimes and sister-bells.
  How I loved my chimes' first ringing!—ring
    they yet o'er Guadalquiver?
I remember when my glass chimes waked the city
    Christmas morning,
  Clear upon the gray morn twilight broke the
    glorious "Adeste."
They were my chimes and I loved them, lightly,
    lovingly I rang them.
  O the silvery clear "Adeste," and the angel-teared
    "venite!"
And the joy of "adoremus!" All the city thronged
    to listen.
  In the silence came the loud cries "Ring again,
    O blessed chimers!"
"Ring," I cried to dark Jacinto who loved not me
    or my glass bells.
  "Not without receiving orders from our Rever-
    end Superior."
"Ring," I cried, and growing frantic with the clam-
    orings of the people,
  I began the great "Adeste." Dark Jacinto moved
    not, rang not.

I would try to ring his part too, but the voice of
    Padre Corso
    Low reproved him; dark Jacinto sullen, hasty
        seized the bell-rope,
Struck my dominant too harshly, broke my glass
    bells, my year's labor.
    Bitter were the words I uttered, and my pride lay
        wounded,—bleeding.
'Twas a melancholy Christmas, but before the
    Infant Jesus,
    I repented all my rash words; and the deep
        humiliation
Seemed as nothing 'neath the mild eyes of the God
    within the manger.
    Penitent I sought the chamber of our reverend
        Novice Master.
Long the kind old man knelt with me, blent our
    voices in contrition;
    Long he spoke of Jesus' meekness, of our glor-
        ious vocation,
Of the eternal years of Heaven, waiting those who
    shall have triumphed.
    Pride was gone and deep contrition sobbed
        throughout my very being.
Ah! that night how calm my slumber, now my soul
    of soul is weary.
    I remember Padre Corso; scarce ten words to me
        he uttered;
Always kind and always silent, always studying or
    writing.
    He was fifty, I was eighteen, he was Priest and I
        was Brother,
Yet my heart's first full affection lay down at his
    feet and perished.
    With the weight of years upon me, with life's
        part almost completed,
I aver that sorrow's sorrow lay in conquering that
    affection.

O'er the wide world I have wandered, and to-night
    my soul is weary.
    O'er my life is incompleteness, o'er my dreams,
        irresolution:
Yet my world of dreams is beauteous as the stars of
    winter mid-night,
    As the coral groves of ocean; as the lordly,
        glacial grandeur
Silent at the feet of ice-bergs, kissed by streamers
    of Aurora.
    In my world of dreams is music, soft as sighs of
        the departed;
Sad as night winds through the hemlocks, sweet as
    dreams of those who love us,
    Troubled as the pulse of ocean, peaceful as the
        Church's amen:
Confident as Catholic christians, when contrite they
    make confession;
    Kind as I would have my heart be towards old
        Earth and all Earth's children.
Ah! my world of song is wondrous! Not for all
    the wide world's treasure,
    Would I part from thee, my dream world, world
        of beauty, world of music!
Nobly pure my realm of dreams is, like the forests
    of the West world
    When frost-spirits weave white mantles, frozen
        foam bands, cirrus cloud webs;
Wreathe each twig of monarch forests in a lace of
    wondrous white-work:
    When frost giants stretch earth's snow-shroud
        down the circular horizon,
And old Winter, white, majestic in the January sun-
    light,
    Loudly claims the palm of beauty from the hand
    of gaudy Summer.

How we love the silent grandeur, found in heart of
    man or in nature!
  Not the glow-light of the valley, but the snow-
    light of the mountain;
Not the heart's great cry of sorrow, but its strong,
    enduring silence.
  Had I been in life as noble as the faces in my
    dream world,—
I had made my death hour peaceful, I had made
    the years eternal
  One long glory;—but I fainted on the peaks of
    self-denial,
Called aloud unto the Human, sought the warm
    lights of the valley.
  Little saw I this old wanderer, when, the eve of
    my Reception,
I knelt through the holy night hours inundated
    with Divine love.
  Stars of January mid-night, sleeping world
    watched by Sierras,
Matin light in monasteries, spires of churches,
    grave of Clothel,
  Duteous rolling Guadalquiver—our great Maker
    calls us brethren!
O the peace of self-denial, the strong joy of Christ's
    beloved!
  Eyes of Calvary smiled o'er me, for my inmost
    soul was stainless.
Then how peacefully I slumbered, but to-night my
    soul is weary.

III.

In my world of dreams is sorrow, pure as mem-
    ories of angels;
  There are dying eyes that loved me, there are
    lonely graves in Moscow:

Rest, O blue eyed Russian woman, friend and
    sweet-heart, wife and sister,
  Slumber 'neath the Russian snow-storm, with our
    pale child on thy bosom!
Pretty pale child, never waken; earth holds not thy
    dark eyes' answer;
  Warm and kind thy mother's arms are, angel
    gentle her affection.
Lo! a tear from earth's old wanderer falls upon the
    graves in Moscow.
  Lo! a tear from earth's old wanderer mingles
    with the waves of ocean
Where she lies, the dead musician, silent lies earth's
    sweetest singer;
  How majestic the Atlantic! Like eternity its
    grandeur!
Like the hand of Fate, colliding crashed the great
    ship on our vessel;
  Like a hell let loose, the waters glared with flame-
    red eyes of swimmers,
Eyes of horror, shrieks of anguish; and when Death
    was satiated,
  Life called back her unconscious children, but
    she called not our musician.
O'er thee shell harps murmur requiem, 'neath the
    storm world, requiescas!
  Lo! a tender sigh is wafting to the pines of
    Arizona
Where we laid the blue-eyed Scotch boy far from
    home and waiting mother;
  O'er thee tall trees murmur requiem, blue-eyed
    rover, requiescas!
Lo! a sigh for far Australia, for a stately home in
    Melbourne;
  For the high romantic young heart who would
    share the actor's fortune,

Self-willed girl who plunged to ruin that lamented
   to receive her.
   I had saved her but she would not, broken-
      hearted, requiescas!
Ah, the dead in memory's grave-yard, the gray
   crosses of a long life!
   Ere I leave my realm of sorrow I would question
      of the unknown
If a cross marked "Padre Corso" rests beside the
   Guadalquiver?
   He is dead, my heart's first idol; he was old
      then, I am old now;
He is dead to earth but living where the poet heart
   is happy.
   In my bosom are his writings, whence I learned
      the mighty flood tides
Underneath that calm exterior, bound down in
   that strong endurance.
   "Farewell, let us meet in Heaven," said the kind
      heart when we parted.
May we meet there! Tenderest tear-drop steal away
   to Guadalquiver.

IV.

O the music of my dream world! Symphonies of
   majestic measure,
   In their strong unanswered longing growing
      mystic, weird, unearthly,
Tinkling, dying in the star world, in the strong
   arms of Orion.
   Stars of beauty, stars of duty, teach us to be
      strong as you are.
Waiting! Waiting! life is waiting. Minor mazes
   faintly breaking
   Weirdly moan like ocean signals, cry like flame-
      ships on dark waters.

Waken dirges, slowly, sadly as the alto moan of
    requiems
Wailed in mid-night monasteries, while six
    candles light the dead monk,
Light the vows clasped in the cold hands, light the
    still face of my dead love.
Would that I to-night were lying in that mid-
    night monastery.
Would to God I had been victor on the peaks of
    self-denial!
Thro' the requiem bells are ringing with a sound
    like tears of angels,
Sweeter than my chimes "Adeste," rising heaven-
    ward, rising homeward,
And they bear my own contrition, bear the
    prayer with which I wrought them
When I tempered the bell-metal, when I fashioned
    them and formed them.
Can it be that God is calling with the voice cast
    in the bell-mould?
Saving me earth's erring wanderer with the nov-
    ice's contrition?
Bells that ruined, bells that save me, ring ye yet
    o'er Guadalquiver?
Bless ye now the sleeping city with the angelus
    of mid-night?
Ah! my fervor, my contrition, my prayer moulded
    in the metal,
"Speak to hearts of Calvary's sorrow, speak in
    accents of contrition."
All the day this prayer I uttered, set it in the hot
    bell metal;
And my dominant I tempered with the tones of love
    and mercy.
"Ring, O bell, across the wide world, ring of
    God's great love and mercy!"
All the day this prayer I murmured, set it in the
    hot bell-metal;

41

And the spirit of the third bell was the promises
of Heaven.
"Ring, O bell, across the wide world ring God's
promises of Heaven!"
All the day this prayer I uttered set it in the hot
bell metal.
Then I gave away the merit of, perhaps, a century's
ringing.
Gave my "Promises of Heaven" sweetest toned,
to Padre Corso,
Gave my second to the people who should listen to
its ringing;
For myself I kept "Contrition." Ring for me, O
gray "Contrition!"
Then a happy, holy novice in the silence of Retreat
time,
In Retreat for my Reception, thus nine days I
prayed and labored.

V.

In my dream world stands Religion, yes the Cath-
olic Religion.
True I've travelled many mazes, winding from
metempsychosis,
Thro' Aristotelian forests, thro' Platonic wilder-
nesses,
Thro' the Eclectic creed of Sybils, of the mystic
Syrian Gnostics,
The great Pantheistic breathings, the wild hopes of
Zoroaster,
Thro' the existent transmigration found in mon-
asteries of Buddha,
Thro' the thunderings of Luther, the development
of Darwin,—
Yet thro' all my orphan heart cried, "Speak to
me, O speak, my Father;
To the unknown God these creeds rise, I would
know Thee,—Maker,—Father!"

'Twas in western Pennsylvania, in the weary days of
    Autumn,
    That I rested from my labors in a fair suburban
        village.
Church there was and cemetery,—half the place was
    cemetery,
    And serene the sky bent o'er the sleepers of the
        Smoky City.
Hourly rose the pick of sexton, daily came the long
    procession,
    Hearse of ermine, hearse of sable; while the great
        heart lamentation
Daily pierced the waiting silence o'er the dead of
    Smoky City.
    'Twas a morning when white frost mist, like the
        winding shroud of Summer,
Kissed and killed the tender dahlias, the chrysan-
    themums and asters;
    Left them wilted sapless sentinels at the obsequies
        of Summer.
To the cries of birds migrating, all the dead leaves
    rustled dirges;
    To the weary "Waiting" written in the mist, the
        sky, the silence,
Each white finger pointed coldly, muttered ghost-
    like, "we are waiting."
    To the restlessness of nature, to the bitterness of
        old hearts,
Came the church bells' tolling, tolling; roll of car-
    riage, clank of horse-hoofs,
    Funeral train kissed by the white mist, hearse of
        sable at the church door.
'Twas this morning that some spirit, winging from
    far Guadalquiver,
    Led me where the unceasing lamp burns, where
        Madonna waits and welcomes.

Forth came one from God's tribunal,—well I knew
    the peace of pardon;
  I had followed, I had knelt there, I had known
    the peace of pardon;
But a mocking, scornful demon rose from out my
    years of wandering,
  Chilled the feeling, veiled the occasion, and I
    watched the priest departing.
Sadly as a soul lamenting what it sought to save
    and could not,
  Rose the prelude wail of Requiem, moaned the
    Kyrie Eleison.
Slowly up the aisle they bore her, placed her where
    the six wax candles
  Mocked the lilies, mocked the black pall o'er the
    dear, dead wife and mother.
Memory murmured with the Requiem, "Rest, O
    blue eyed Russian woman!"
  Faith from out the depths of Reason murmured
    "Kyrie Eleison;"
Prostrate, broken lay my proud heart murmuring
    Kyrie Eleison.
  "Dies Irae," wailed the organ, but I heard not
    "Dies Irae."
Heard only the voice of Jesus calling to the erring
    wanderer,
  Calling with the voice of Clothel, with the smile
    of Padre Corso;
Old prayers rose in old time measures, old tears
    trembled in contrition;
  All the novice heart awakened 'neath the years of
    change and error,
Wakened humble, contrite, hopeful, waiting for the
    peace of pardon
  That shall fall as benediction o'er the penitent's
    confession;
And it came,—God's absolution, God's abiding
    benediction.

Thro' the Winter I remained as organist of the
great church organ.
How I played my own life-story in the long, still
hours of practice.
Almost human seemed the organ, with a human
love I loved it;
How it rose and trembled, waiting like my own
irresolution;
How it sank in soft inertness from the combat, the
grand "forte;"
Scorning effort, scorning victory, in a strife that is
unworthy.
Sadder, holier, rose the organ in the chords of
life's affections;
Yet there rose the strains in sequence of God's
promises to mortals,
And the great "amen" was peaceful as the Presence on the altar.

Ever restless is the spirit. I departed from the
village,
I re-entered the world-maelstrom when the
churches chimed Adeste.
Pain of heart and deep soul-longing backward
turned to Guadalquiver;
To my glass bells, dark Jacinto, gentle Brothers,
holy Fathers;
Kind dark eyes that smiled upon me, heavenly peace
of Christ's beloved.
Hallowed monastery memories with the churches
chimed Adeste.

Mist and rain hung o'er the village on the morn
that I departed.
Thro' the accustomed path I wandered mid the
dead of Smoky City.

'Neath the rain a covered wagon hastened toward
   the pauper's corner.
  " 'Tis the murderer, Giovanni, he was hanged at
     nine this morning."
"Happy corse the rain rains over!" Time's sad
   product, requiescas.
  Thro' the rain a snow-white hearse came, but no
     mourning carriage followed.
Ah! the lonely baby coffin in the strong arms of the
   sexton;
  Lower, lower, baby, wake not; muddy clods fall
     o'er your cradle,
Narrow, cold, your mother's arms are; you are
   happy that you wake not.
  It is well that Heaven should weep thus o'er the
     sad homes of her children,
O'er the head-stones of the dead ones, o'er the
   house tops of the living;
  These long tears will ease the spirit, and the night
     stars shall be peaceful.
In my own night stars are rising; stars of pity, stars
   of promise.
  Nobler are the star-affections than the passion
     lights of morning,
Mellower are the hues of Autumn than of inexper-
   ienced Spring-time,
  And the old considerate mountains hide the
     errors of the valley.
So the heart of man grows kinder as the deep life-
   years pass o'er him,
  So the heart of man grows broader, knowing
     human strength and weakness,
Knowing pain and all the evils that shall come upon
   the living;
  Till the heart is grandly human like the heart of
     Prince Siddartha,
Nay, until the heart is god-like with the expiring
   love of Jesus.

46

PART THIRD

When shall care and pain be ended?
   Were I he who rules Creation
I would utter, " Let the end come!" Cease the
   writhing tide of evil,
   Cease the wailing of the women, cease the
   anguish of the strong man.
Weary are the sultry cities where the voices of the
   children
   Catch the moan of factory motion and the long
   lament of labor.
Youth is unreal, life is hollow, every human heart
   is weary;
   All the weary world is calling, "Let the end come!
   Let the end come!"
Failure life, the end is coming. Calm upon the
   Guadalquiver,
   To the happy scenes of childhood, they are bear-
   ing old Lionel.
Glorious sunset skies bend o'er him; reverently the
   dark eyes open,
   Smile upon the approaching steeples, on the old
   familiar places.
Lo! the gleaming of the grave stones, and the statue
   of Madonna
   Which had raised the hand to bless him in the
   Forty Hours' procession.
Lo! the grand old monastery, hallowed home of
   Padre Corso.
   Childhood's tears rise in the dim eyes of the old
   man, suffering, dying.
Said the Spanish priest beside him, " Aged wan-
   derer, you are dying;
   Is your soul at peace with Heaven? May I give
   you absolution?
Dark-eyed stranger, you are dying. Ere the sun's
   refracted glories

Shall have sunk 'neath the Sierras, you will be
beyond the sunset,"—
"I shall be beyond the sunset,—I shalll know what
life and death are."
Wake, O angelus of evening, with a sound like
tears of angels!
"Bells! my bells! the bells I moulded,—Hark! my
"Promises of Heaven,"
That I gave to Padre Corso, and my own, my own
"Contrition!"
I am dying and I fear not,—Hark, my own, my
own Contrition!
I love God, and— Death embraced him 'neath
the sounds of absolution,
And the echoes lingering, dying of the "Promises of
Heaven."

MORTUA EST.

Cold is the heart—burned out in the youth conflagration.

I have stood by the grave of Petrarch and Laura; I have beheld the rock whence Sappho flung herself into the wave; I have seen the name, "Leonora D'Este" traced by the hand of Tasso; I have stood among the silent nobility of Pere la Chaise and Westminster,—I am standing by her grave.

In the sister-shadow of this grave, all other graves become sacred; in the sister light of this love, all other loves become hallowed; in the sister glory of this soul, all other souls become holy. O the grave of one we loved so long ago! How the well known date on the head-stone seems to turn a thorn lying painless in the soul! How the name breathed again on our lips conjures forth a vision whose mournful eyes watch us out of the Past,—ay, and reproach us! Here we recall kind words that were spoken, kind actions done; perhaps, too, we recall hasty actions and words that brought tears to the eyes closed so long. O Child! would you avoid the anguish of this memory, be warned in time; now, in the troubled life of every day be kind to the dear ones at home. Lover, husband, wife! would you avoid the anguish of this memory, wound not the heart that loves you. Affection is a holy thing and with the magnanimity of a god, it gives into your hands the darts, fixed in its own life-blood, that you may wound it, kill it when you will.

O the grave! the grave! Here lies a little child who would walk to the swans at rest on the lake and who saw not the death-arms around them. Wondrous golden head, beauteous blue eyes, rosy

49

boy, who would touch the white swans at rest on the lake, and who died in the death arms around them. Little sleeper, rest. Earth's first deception was for thee its last.

Here he lies who wronged me years ago. Does a thought of bitterness rise on beholding the pompous mound and the carved name coldly defiant? No, he who has died, has expiated all wrongs to mortals. Earth's heaviest wrongs can ask no atonement greater than that of the humiliating agony of death. Earth's fiercest heart subsiding thro' the years may stand in pity, even in prayer, by the grave of one who wronged it years ago.

Shall I turn away as one without hope? "Expecto resurrectionem mortuorum et vitam venturi saeculi." "I expect the resurrection of the dead and the life of the world to come." Somehow the gray night gathering o'er the world becomes holy when those words are spoken. The snows fall more tenderly. The white blankets muffle more kindly the sleepers in Death's dormitory. The human heart, as tho' it had heard a voice from its native Heaven, feels nobler, feels truer to that which is worthiest within us, when those words are spoken. Human hearts, cherish them! Winds of Winter, murmur them thro' branches of leafless trees. Snowflakes falling, whisper them over the world; over the tomb of Petrarch and Laura, over St. Mary's, Greenwood, Pere la Chaise,—over her grave.

HARP ECHOES.

Yes, I came back to the old home to-day;
   I paused at the door-way,—she used to stand there;
I knew I must suffer, I tried to be strong,
   I entered the parlor and sank in—her chair.

The veins of my throat were as strong bursting
    strings,
  Their tension relaxed with the gathering tear:
I looked to our God, and I tried to be strong—
  But I gazed on the picture she painted last year.

In corridor, stair-way, and desolate hall
  I miss her, I miss her; before me I see
The place where she painted, the place where she
    played,
  But her voiceless piano is mourning with me.

I knelt in the chapel, God's blessing was there,
  I prayed to the silent Heart caring for all;
I almost touched peace in that depth of the deep,
  But the storm spirit shuddered o'er her vacant
    stall.

The many lights glimmered, sweet incense arose;
  God waited to bless us with gleams of our goal;
Some hand touched her organ, and all the world
    moaned,
  O Sister, my Sister, peace, peace to thy soul!

II.

Out of the many I sought that one,
  And Death sought that one, too;
The white cross tells who the victory won,
  And the grave is between me and you.—
O my lost one, rest in peace
  Where the sounds of sorrow cease!

Out of the grave I feel your hand,
  I hear your laugh as of yore;
Your music lures to the better land,
  And the grave is the grave no more.—
O my lost one, rest in peace
  Where the sounds of sorrow cease!

Still is the organ that waked for you,
    That throbbed your pleasure or pain;
Hushed is the master minstrelsy,
    I never shall hear it again.—
O my lost one, rest in peace
    Where the sounds of sorrow cease!

From sweet violin the spirit is fled,
    From harp and from silvery horn:
O world of Song, the musician is dead,
    Then mourn, mourn, mourn!

Have you approached the Master of Song
    Whence the choirs of spheres have birth?
Have you forgotten the key-note of wrong,
    And the dissonant chords of earth?
O my lost one, rest in peace
    Where the sounds of sorrow cease!

Cold little hand in the grave to-night,
    The music world feels your thrill;
The queen of Sorrow stands robed in white
    Where the children of Song are still:

She takes in her hand your own violin,
    Your harp and your silvery horn;
The children of Song her strain begin,
    And mourn, mourn, mourn.

Hark! from the prelude of sorrow is prayer;
    The Requiem Mass is sung:
Some seraph of God is celebrant there,
    For the "sanctus" bell is rung.

While "Sanctus, sanctus" hallows all,
    And the bells of angels play;
White wings touch the grave with tender call
    And bear my love away.—
O my lost one! rest in peace
    Where the sounds of sorrows cease.

III.

How is it now in the world of the dead?
    O that your spirit might come
Out from the mystery over the tomb
    And tell of the future home!

Come if you can as I bend o'er your grave,
    Tell me your spirit is free;
Tell me you rest with the choirs of the blest
    And you wait for the earth-loves and me.

Silence majestic reprovingly mild,
    Bending o'er life's waiting way,
Bids me depart from this grave in my heart
    To the living cry of to-day.

In the heart silence, distinctly I hear
    All the world calling with me,—
"Light us, O Faith! down the shadow of death,
    And shine over life's mystery."

So loud was my own cry I heard not the roar
    Of the wrecks on the sea of pain:
I have sorrowed so long, I will rise and be strong,
    I will clasp hands with Duty again.

IV.

What my heart says,—that I sing.
    Thro' the forest sighing,
The autumn breeze and the bending trees
    Bewail the dead and dying,
Mourn where my love is lying.

All my spirit sobs with these.
    All the leaves of all the trees,
All the holy stars that rise
    Countless in the midnight skies;

Every shrub, and blade of grass,
　Wings of night-birds as they pass,
Every voice of pain or mirth
　Born of Heaven or born of earth,—
Bending o'er that white cross bed,
　Mourn because my love is dead.

While the world mourns, dear musician,
　Hear it not, but sleep;
Tho' in realms of song above thee
　Sister spirits weep.

Tho' all instruments of music
　Mourn their queen with me;
Tho' they wake untouched by mortal
　One long harmony.

Hear it not, O sweetest singer!
　Earthly song with earth retires;
Wings thy spirit rapt exulting,
　Mid the cherub choirs.

V.

I'm used to it now—that pain at my heart;
　And the presence is kind that forevermore glides
Thro' familiar old places, re-living a life
　That forever departing,—forever abides.

I heard music last night. How the old sorrow
　　throbbed
　When her faithless piano awoke in glad strain
To the touch of another! With bitter reproach,
　The human heart called for the lost hand again.

Oh! thrill thro' the mazes of music once more,
　Little hand that touched worlds where the song
　　spirits dwell;
Tinkling rivulets, bending pines, high stars of
　　sound,
　The dirge in the deep,—the eternal farewell;

The moonlight came down at thy call; and the sea
  Told to thee its regret, its deep throbbings of
    pain:
They will come never more, they are calling with
    me
  "Little hand in the grave, come again, come
    again!

VI.

O music, be still! Shall I ever be strong?
  Shall I ever clasp duty, and walk hand in hand
From the pain central self, down the broad human
    strand
    That silently leads toward the lone silent land.

O sad sister world! you are stronger than I;
  I watch you with pitying pain.
I hear not a cry where the broken hearts lie,
  Nor a sigh from the world-weary brain.

VII.

The lightning revels thro' the primal grove;
  Cloud to cloud is calling.
Replete with sound the fiery arrowy path.
  Midway rains are falling;—
Falling over her grave.
  The lightning is flashing,
The thunder is crashing,
  The wild storm is dashing,
Maddest where the tall trees wave,
  Saddest over her grave.

Thro' the cold window pane,
  See how earth mourns her loss!
The trees that knew her wail again,
  The heavens sob in tearful rain,
The heart that loves her cries in pain
  Over that still gray cross.

O sister soul! you are not there,
    The dust to dust is given;
The immortal part, the noble heart
    Is happy now in Heaven.

And I shall meet you when my hour shall come
    To pass in dread transition to that state
Which we believe to be the soul's true home,
    Where Christ and all the good of ages wait.

I think there 'll be reproach upon your face
    That I have grieved ignobly for your loss,
And borne a dead light thro' the halls of life,
    And signed even duty with your iron cross.

The pain I could not help; but the lament
    Is useless. And the good I might have done
Lies tangled, dead in mournful memories;
    And high ideals from my life are gone. ·

Yet might I rise on all ennobling pain
    And call them back, out from the realm of youth,
And look them firmly in the face again,
    And love them better in the robes of truth!

Yet might I be what I have longed to be,—
    The noble heart, the generous, the true;
Whose love is universal charity,
    Whose life is for the good that it can do!

VIII.

They are singing of beauty and youth,
    They are praising the brave and the bold,
They are singing of honor and truth,
    And of love that shall never grow old.

They are singing of those who roam,
  They are praising the stars of even,
They are singing the pleasures of home,
  They are singing the hopes of Heaven.

One sings of the sad billows' roll,
  Of the sorrows asleep in the sea;
One sings of the longing of soul
  That watches o'er life's mystery.

We are singing of sister and brother,
  Singing of those who roam;
Singing of father and mother,
  Singing of childhood's home.

We are singing of birds that are flown;
  We are singing old age and its gloom:
The music is murmuring in sorrow's low tone,
  And the lover laments o'er the tomb.

I touch the chords of submission,
  I sigh with the sobbing wave;
I sing to the dead musician
  Low in the gray-cross grave.

We touch the chords of submission;
  We sigh with the sobbing wave:
Each sings to some dead musician
  Down in the lone heart-grave.

IX.

  Mighty waves of music start;
  There is hunger in my heart.

Just a year ago to-night
  Since I knelt by her side;
Darkness tingeing all of light
  As she died.

Sounds are sighing olden woe,
She is lying cold and low.

They are playing airs she played
    On the gay violin.
Do they know my heart will break
    With the strain?

        All my being cries in pain,
        "Dead musician, come again!"

Sing in silence, stars of even,
    Bid the players cease;
Give my soul the hopes of Heaven,
    Give me peace.

X.

It is raining over her grave,
    And the winds are wearily wailing;
And the trees like broken manhood wave
    Forever near forever unavailing.

A year ago to-day they buried her.
    Of all unheeding,
I stand alone in the storm.
    My heart is bleeding.

A year in the world of the dead,
    A year embraced by the tomb;
A year have the knights of the charnel house fed
    On the lips that I loved in their bloom.

Music is borne on the lulling rain.
    O cold little head, lie low!
Tho' the wind and the rain with the music of pain
Loudly lament that you come not again,
    And tears of affection flow.

XI.

Sweet is the voice of song,
 Sweet are the strains we sung,
Meaningless, mystic music that we sung
 When we were young.

Strange is the voice of song,
 When other lips repeat
Words that are sacred for the sake of one
 Who made life sweet.

Sad is the voice of song,
 When on a foreign shore,
Strange lips are singing what our loved shall sing,
 Ah—nevermore!

XII.

I have learned a useful lesson
 From the years,
And if you to-night behold me
 Bowed in tears;
'Tis not that the winds of winter
 O'er her rave;
But for every human heart cry
 O'er a grave.

For the cold face at the window
 While the storm is wild,
Turning from the empty cradle
 Of her child.

For the first great grief that calls loud
 O'er the waiting bed,
Mother, mother! O my mother!
 You are dead!

For the ghost-like rooms that knew her,
    For the altered homes;
For the hollow world that is waiting
    Till she comes.

I have learned a useful lesson
    From the years,
And if you to-night behold me
    Bowed in tears,
'Tis not that my soul is sobbing,
    "Let the striving cease!"
But because the world is crying,
    "Give us peace!"

XIII.

A glitter of the old glow
    Fell upon my heart;
They sang the songs of long ago
    And made the old tears start.
I left the merry party,
    The midnight city slept;
The longing silence sighed with me
    And all my spirit wept.
O sleepers of the city!
    Our sorrow soon shall cease;
Our God shall smile in pity,
    And give us peace.

XIV.

I have bid old memories sever
    From the homes in which they dwell;
I have said farewell forever,
    Low and long I said farewell.

All my soul of soul is weeping
    Folded in the arms of Pain;
As I stand where thou art sleeping,
    I shall never stand again.

I shall sail away to-morrow,
  I shall wake 'neath foreign skies;
I shall drift o'er tides of sorrow
  To our waiting paradise.

Other songs may soothe my sadness,
  Other eyes may wait for me;
I shall see the smile of gladness,
  Thine again I shall not see.

I shall hear the organ swelling
  Thro' the master minstrelsy;
I shall hear all music telling
  Of a grave beyond the sea.

"Dust thou art, to dust returnest!"
  Never wails where thou dost dwell;
Life is calling strong and earnest—
  Low and long and last—farewell.

AL RIDER.

"Out of the depths have I cried to Thee!" So Pythagoras, Kepler, Newton cried—out of the depths of Thought. How God-like are those depths; and how few there are that find them! There are the diamond beds of life,—there are the fountain-heads of streams which have blessed the world. The names which star-like glitter in the firmament of each art and science, are the names of those who have labored in the dusky mines of Thought. Slow, heavy, analytical, all-comprehensive Thought is the mathematical accuracy of Euclid and of Pythagoras; the logical lucidity of Aristotle; the flame-light of Dante's Inferno: ay, the captured spirit breathing forth from all that is worthy in painting, sculpture, poetry, and music; the liberated spirit rushing forth in man's inventions; the miracle worker, the all possible one, walking upon the waters; searching the clouds; flashing across the world from shore to shore.

Thought is the great pacificator. Only analyze deeply enough, and all perplexities, sorrows, wrongs of earth resolve themselves into their harmless elements. With eyes fixed on God; and holding a scroll unrolling out from the past and losing itself in the future, Thought watches over the troubled to-day and cries, "Peace!"

Thought is soul-music. Have the creations of genius thrilled us? Have we wept with Lear in the storm, or with Margaret in prison? All things grand in this world are to the hearts that produced them as flame-light to flame. O the painful grandeur of that flame heart! There rise the great pleading eyes of Gautama; there laughs Cleopatra;

there agonizes the love of Tasso; there lies the magical beautiful woe on the dead face of Sappho. Voices steal thro' the flame heart like odors of roses and lilies; voices sob thro' the flame heart as a lost child at the grave of its mother;—and there is music on the river under the stars—soul music.

Thought is God's Sanctum Sanctorum; and all who shall have been found worthy to enter therein shall find the Truth.

The man of the world, the statesman, astronomer, philosopher, poet—Al Rider sat alone in Stelloburgum,—the central glass-domed observatory of Uraniberg. Silence was upon the world. The great waves of the Baltic, in unison with the watching human heart, surged in subdued awe under the stars. Al Rider turned from the optic glass thro' which he had been scanning the heavens. A look of painful unrest gleamed in the deep dark eyes. His was a soul truly royal; his was a mind earnestly striving to see God's placid, eternal truth in the infinitesimal reflection of reason and science; his was a heart—a great Aeolian harp on which, cognizant of their power, the life winds played. Vibrations answered a zephyr, and maddening melody, frenzy re-echoed their pleasure and pain.

The mocking, victorious stars, seeming to deride his impotence, looked full upon him. A light wind blew down his latest optic glass, and it lay shattered at his feet. Something in the politic glitter of the glassy fragments seemed to reflect the laughing mockery of the stars. The human mind was weary and the poet heart sank deep—deep in thought: "My senses perceive thee, O earth home, O starry worlds! The effect pre-supposes a cause; the thing made, a Maker. That Cause, that Maker, that God, where art Thou? What art Thou? Does it seem well to imprint on the soul a question which cannot be answered? Yet should that world creating Intelligence pause to answer me? Yes, since He created me with a desire to know, a capability of suffering. Should He come in God-head splendor, could the clayey wormling live? Nay, something in us, but not all in us, can see God and live. How the little hearts of men would wither in the All-Light! But the kindness of life, the earnest seeking for truth, the soul-longings for the beautiful, the good—shall these grow dark in the All-Light? Nay, rather shall they rush therein and rest.

Truth where art thou? I have sought thee long. Mohammed knew thee not; Buddha on the heights of human kindness beheld thee veiled and tearful. Christ—is it not earth's best? He answers the heart He made, the heart with a desire to know, with a capability of suffering. He came not in God-splendor so that in his presence the clayey wormling writhed and stung and lived.

Are not His teachings life's grandest? Like the beneficent sunlight, they shine o'er the wide creation, and no atom of life is unwarmed by their beam. Unto the children they come, and, smiling, they bless them; unto the wretched they come, and, with hand caressing, they bend over the sorrowing soul. The Time-storm stands rebuked. The billows fall, and sobbing roll away, and sighing wander far away; and smiling rippling die away on the eternal shore. Unto the erring they come. With eyes of serious tenderness, with heart of pitying pain they say "Neither do I condemn thee!" Unto the grave they come. O graves of earth, ye bury deep the bodies of the dead and the hearts of the living! Then is it well to stand with Christ's teachings over a grave; yet—"

Approaching footsteps broke the deep abstraction. Al Rider rose as the opening door admitted his two friends, Otho and Kaled. They brought to him from Tycho Brahe a new and still more powerful optic glass; they bore also intelligence concerning a wondrous star located near Caph in the constellation Cassiopeia. This star had suddenly sprung into existence under the startled eye of Tycho Brahe as he sat scanning the heavens. It had rapidly increased in splendor; it shone tonight a star of first magnitude. Al Rider adjusted the glass and gazed long upon the heavens.

The heights are cold. The peaks are alone. Yet on the mountain heights they dwell—earth's sciences, earth's philosophies. Yet on the mountain peaks they dwell, earth's heroes, earth's geniuses. Al Rider watched the heavens. In myriad millions gleamed the stars. The colored stars rejoiced in their beauty; smiled thro' their halos of sapphire, of amber, of crimson, of green. The star clusters trembled with love secure in their vaporous home. Space, time, immensity spoke in the silence

HARP ECHOES.

Waiting,—half our life is spent in waiting;
Here he was to be, and here he is not.
Little truth there is and less of wisdom;
Sealed upon us the capricious future
Opening hour by hour with fates opposing.
Let him come or come not! This is pleasing;
This silent eye of heaven would have me gaze
Within the trackless, awful, vast, concave.
O space, immensity, infinity,
Chaotic order! How the human soul
Stands numb and trembling touching the unknown.
Great Tycho Brahe sits in his lone tower,
Holding this commune while the seasons roll.
Lo! thro' the mazy halled Uraniberg,
Al Rider comes with Kaled by his side.
They stand above the range of common minds,
They raise me to a longing for the true.

65

There is within them sternest principle,
And that which all commanding, elevates.
"Look thro' my optic glass, late ones," I cried,
"A new one, Rider, thro' whose powerful eye
Zel shines resplendent, a new world to-night:
Most brilliant, of first magnitude,—all fire."
He gazed intently on the flaming world;
Grand Rider, whom I love for wealth of soul.
I knew the asking heart unanswered,
The fretting of the soul confined, bound down;
The silent infinite o'er impotence.
"Rider," I cried, and touched him as a child
Might touch a father stern yet much beloved.
"Dear friend, turn from the sullen mystery;
In our Eclectic creed, the Sibyl says
'Tis vain to call the secrets from the stars,
Between us hangs yon vast infinity—"
A groan from Rider, and his lordly head
Sank low a helpless burden on my arm.
From Tycho Brahe at his optic glass
A woeful cry, a heavy sounding fall.
What is it, Kaled?—Kaled, see—the star!
He looked, I looked; but Zel was seen no more:
No more, in all the heavens, that brilliant star.
What had they seen,—the prostrate noble ones?
A fiat of eternity unrolled?
Poor human minds breasting infinity!
Al Rider, rest! if rest be for thy soul.
True Kaled lavished all of chemic lore,
But, thro' the long night hours, that helpless form
Reposed upon my arm; in that embrace
I felt his soul with my soul inter-twined.
The bands of dawn were breaking in the east
        Beyond the glassy domed Uraniberg;
I longed for Truth, true knowledge of the True;
And, as I urged in restlessness of soul,
I bent o'er him akin in mystery
And as I gazed, Al Rider's eyes met mine.

We knew each other's secret and revered.
True Kaled entered with the drugs that heal.
Al Rider discoursed long and reverently:
"We are encompasséd by mystery;
That we know nothing is our truest creed;
Yet something in us calls to the unknown
And claims affinity beyond the stars."
A silence fell oppressive, and the sea
Moaned in the heavy darkness fraught with pain,
A chilling wind played thro' Al Rider's hair.
I knelt beside him, Kaled nearer drew
And spoke of union with immortal Brahm,
Reunion of the spark unto the flame.
"Mohammed says there is no God, but God
And he is mighty, patient, loving all
And Jesus Christ says we shall rise again
Lo! our Eclectic creed is fraught with hope!"

Al Rider

We have of all creeds chosen their better part,
And cleansed it fully from its base alloy,
And yet, like Buddha, till I gain that state
Where memory unfolds all that has been,
A universal knowledge viewed from Brahm—
An exile I,—

Kaled

An exile I,

Otho

And I.

Al Rider

This night yon brilliant star burst in the heavens,
And nearer, nearer came a flaming world.
And lo! it burst, it scattered, it grew dark.
Did Tycho fall! He saw the wondrous change.
From this night forth I view the heavens no more:
I wander far, and if I do return
I shall have found that which all mortals crave
Peace, peace of soul, and knowledge of the True.

Not in the human creed, the common throng,
Perfidious, all-self,—not there—not there;
Far, far away 'tween nature and the soul.
"The universe is God;" the Pantheist says;
Nay but God permeates the solemn wilds,
And, if the soul be amply purified,
This God may touch me and I shall be pure.

Otho.

Al Rider, Stelloburgum is no more
For me or Kaled if you be not here.
Where would you go, Al Rider? for the True
Is sealed beyond the grave.

Al Rider

       Then I go there.
I know you would dissuade me, but my mind
Stands as Polaris in the winter sky.
What answer, Kaled? Will you seek the true?

Kaled.

Yes o'er the alembic and the crucible.

Al Rider

Then do we search?

Kaled.

Aye, search for twenty years.

Al Rider

       For life—

Otho

Beyond life ere you find the goal.

Al Rider

Beyond life—See yon gray necropolis,
A link apparent in a chain unknown!
How the young day caresses the gray slabs.
The shadows yield; the mystic ilex trees
Stand sentinel and murmur requiem.

Kaled

How the blue hills cloud capped salute the morn!

Otho.

The world is fair viewed from a mind in peace.
Here is a silhouette of Augustine.
Behold, Al Rider, in his face dwells peace.

Al Rider

'Tis calm but calm that speaks a tempest passed
Grand serious head and face that typifies
A master mind contemplating the True.

Otho.

Grand Augustine! Rememberest thou his words;
"The soul is restless till it rests in God.

Al Rider.

The goal we know, the path there we know not;
But we will know. When we shall meet again
'Twill be in knowledge and deep peace of soul;
From virtue's pinnacle our souls shall gaze
Upon the infinite, eternal Truth.

Kaled and Otho.

From virtue's pinnacle! So let it be.

Al Rider

When we have gained that star now lost as Zel
Resort to far Chartreuse. We stand to-day
Upon the self-same spot; oh! far removed
From virtue's pinnacle. Let us ascend!

Kaled and Otho.

It shall be so, and we shall meet again.

Al Rider.

And now farewell!

Kaled and Otho.

Al Rider, fare thee well.

"Resort to far Chartreuse." Al Rider said,
Lo! I have found the True, and I have come
To greet those friends who, twenty years ago,
Stood on that base with me; oh! far removed
From virtue's height and knowledge of the True.
Al Rider, Kaled, 'tis your Otho calls—
A white haired, broken pilgrim. Wild Chartreuse,
My wearied limbs refuse to bear me on,
Here I must rest. The face of God is dark,
The star above Jerusalem is lost,
And storm is dark'ning in the sullen sky.
O Thou, whose head the mountain bed received,
Whose lips, the dews of sad Gethsemani,
Whose weary limbs, the all supporting Cross—
Look down upon me; smile across the gloom!
I wandered on, the smile of God returned.
Before me rose an entrance to some den
Of man or beast, and, lo! I stood within
A desert cave some Bruno may have trod.
I knelt in prayer and prayed for Heaven's rest,
And o'er my cry the waiting angels sang,
" 'Twill not be long, old heart, 'twill not be long!"
The storm burst forth in madness o'er the wild,
The lightning reveled on the mountain brow,
And in its glare a human figure stood.
I hurried toward him, brought him to my cave.
"Art thou a man of God?" Then pray with me.
(The silence of the desert may not speak.)
We knelt together, while the tempest raved
While crashing trees fell round us, and the waste
A mighty grandeur rolled in living light.
Old forms exhausted sank secure in God.
A beauteous morn was breaking o'er the world,

But sobbing trees and chilling winds might speak
The recent revel of the elements.
The stranger slept, gaunt recluse, and I rose
To gather herbs and roots for sustenance;
Returning laden, I first fairly saw
The stranger of the storm. Thro' time's disguise,
Thro' ravages of change, thro' chill of soul—
We saw, we recognized—and we knelt down.
"Yet Kaled, speak!"

Kaled

Fair Otho, is it thou?

Otho

Old Otho now. Then thou hast found the True?

Kaled

Deep peace is ours and knowledge of the True.

Otho

The earth stain lingers on this gleam of Heaven
Al Rider comes not. May our best have failed?

Kaled.

'Tis ours to pray for him and trust our God.

Otho.

Al Rider, oh! my soul writhes in its God:
If thou art lost, if our eternity
Shall roll between thy God-like soul and God!

Kaled.

A saint awaiting Heaven dwells in Chartreuse;
We'll gain his prayers for our Al Rider's soul.
He wrote the words which brought me to my God,
An exile in the far America—

Otho.

America! O Kaled, speak thy part,
Thy devious path thro' twenty weary years.

Kaled.

The heights secured, the heavy stairs may fall.

Otho.

Yet gazing down were food for gratitude.

Kaled's Story.

Strange fortune called me to Arabia.
Al Bershid wrote to me in glowing words
Of wondrous workings in his laboratory;
Of strange conversions, powerful sublimates;
And magic transformations—allotropes.
    "A thosand substances apparent, few
The elements; and, in our alcahest,
We gain the elements of gold and life;
Then combinations, allotropic forms
Must give us silver, gold, and human life.
Come to Arabia, come and search with me
The far quintessence, the all-spirit lost."
I sought the alchemist, and dreamed his dream,
And o'er the alembic and the crucible,
O'er acids, vapors, metal-elements,
O'er compounds analyzed and synthesized,
O'er elements combined in every form
By distillation, sublimation, chance
Of cold, heat, sunlight, freed affinities—
For fifteen years we sought for gold and life.
Proportion, depth of mind and breadth of soul
Repaid our efforts, but we formed not gold.
We found the herbs that nourish human life,
All herbs medicinal and friend to man—
We sought "elixir vitae."   Antidotes
And many compounds bringing aid to man
And drugs oblivious found we,—but not life.

A sympathetic ink we chanced to form:
Al Beshid called it symbol of our lives
Whose works lie cold to blossom forth in Brahm.

One day as weary, heartsore, I gazed far
Upon a scene of noonday loveliness
I saw a beautious child whose merry laugh
Re-echoed thro' the white pimento trees,
And swept the chord of joy within each heart.
A woman's voice arose in wild despair,
The fair child prostrate lay, the venom clasp
Of Egypt's serpent wound about his life.
With antidotes and soporific drugs
I reached the child, the serpent raised his head
And knew in me his deadly enemy.
Without a change of eye-glare long we gazed,
But I exhaled, from a replenished case,
A soporific, and I knew its power.
The child lay sleeping in the cold embrace,
The anguished mother knew no more her pain.
I sank not, for I used reactive fumes:
At length the serpent lay in truce with life.
I quickly disengaged it from the child,
And placed it in a chloral vat to die.
Before the child awakened I annulled,
With antidotes, all venom in the wound;
Then binding herbs medicinal, I stood
Contemplating a life that I had saved.
No hour of fifteen years had joy for me
Like this—the silent bliss of doing good;
I felt that I had almost touched the True.

Henceforth to seek it in the public good!
To place on fevered lips the cooling draught.
To strengthen weakness. O'er the withering pain
To wave the love wand of oblivion.
Unto disease and sin and misery
In dungeons, hospitals, on battle-fields
To come with love and healing! Wondrous
        thought!
May virtue's pinnacle be charity?

The mother woke with sad remembering cry.
I brought to her the child. She stupefied
Fell at my feet in wordless gratitude.
I turned away, lamenting that of life
So far exhausted, 'twas my first true deed:
Henceforward I should live for good alone.

A few days later, strong in purpose true
I stood departing for the busy town
To seek disease; to mitigate all pain.
Aaron, my Arab courser, knelt for me,
And I was on my mission proudly borne.

I've failed to vivify life-elements;
Yet may it be that some far origin
Evolves creative essence, and that life
Is emanative of the Intelligence
That guides the stars, and rules infinity?
Capella reigns to-night and Procyon,
Arcturus trembles faintly in the East,
Orion waits in world-like majesty,
Apollo, Thuban, Sirius, Betelguise,
Polaris, Caph,—the vacant bed of Zel,—
Dear lights of Stelloburgum, ye are fair!
Our great Al Rider, have you found the True?
My path has failed; and virtue's pinnacle
Is lost as Zel. All life, all space, all time,
Some vast eternal Intellect controls.
We dream of Brahm. Is Brahm intelligence?
And is my soul a spark of Brahmic flame?
May yon Omnipotence have smiled o'er me
That would compel his secrets? I recall
The vulgar wonder when by occult power,
We held Al Bershid in the empty air.
Now had some clown, to whose dull intellect
Our art unknown, might never be made known,
Essayed to imitate; with what contempt,
Security, derision, had we gazed!

Yet were that clown the work of our own hands
A part of our full being—could we hate?
Nay, nature teaches that we love our own.

The dream of doing good I realized;
My Aaron bore me o'er a waiting world;
And pain and grim disease fled at our call,
And death came down oblivious o'er the strife.
Unto old age, whose ills no man may cure,
We gave the balm of hope and healing words.
But ever restless is the human heart.
They spoke to me of far America,
The founts of Youth; De Soto's lordly bed,
The trackless grandeur of the Indian land.
So faithful Aaron, my one friend and love,
Stood by my side upon the sailing boat
That sought the stranger wave and stranger shore.
Proud Aaron, with what tossings, restless neighs
He trod his confines 'tween the sea and sky,
And reared, receding from the treacherous wave,
As tho' he saw it yielding,—claiming him
And felt the embraces of his grave to be.
The morning of the eighteenth day arose
Upon a breathless void, a waveless sea.
Asleep lay ocean in the zone of calms.
Our vessel lay as moveless as a raft
Beheld on great tar lake of Trinidad.
All day the glass eternal rippled not;
While men grew desperate, and offered it
Shoes, watches, books, plates, boxes, swords,—
And smiled to see one thankless bubble rise;
Gray night came down, and man retired to dream
Of clouds, of rolling waves, of mighty winds.
Gray morn arose, and man awoke to see
A burned out sky, a peace—how terrible!
The glare, the gloom; but not the strife of Hell.
Yet seven days passed; the captain came with hope.
"A cloud appeared far in the eastern sky,
And were our burden lighter we might sail;

Beside, the last of our provisions failed
For yonder steeds; to-morrow they must stand
Sick, fearful, starving. 'Twere humanity
To cast them in the deep and save the ship.
Himself would sacrifice eight noble steeds,
He asked his generous hearted passengers
To merge self-interest in the common good.
"Take mine," they said, "take mine," they said,
    .   "take mine,"
"Take Aaron, my white Arab Aaron, too!"
'Twas twilight. And the deck led to the wave
A lame, old horse, blindfolded walked thereto
The slide drew back, he struggled in the calm
Sank, rose with head uncovered. Fiery eyes
Sank watching us from out their waiting grave.
A terror gathered in the living herd;
Short, piteous cries rose; fiery fearful eyes
That asked a human sympathy. I thought
Of transmigration and cold, shuddering turned
To leave it all; but Aaron knelt for me,
And eyes of meek intelligence met mine.
I threw my arms around his neck and cried.
Old gray beard!—yet my very being cried.
"My faithful one, my beauteous one, my true!
Is't thus that I repay fidelity!
Poor trembling one!" I heard the frequent splash.
A hand touched mine. I led my Aaron forth.
"My Aaron, we must part." A fresh cool breeze
Rose o'er my sacrifice. Upon the slide,
The slide withdrawn; a sick'ning heavy splash—
(Yon albatross seemed biting at my heart.)
The vessel quivered, caught the approaching storm
While lightning, thunder, winds, and mighty rain
Raved over Aaron as the vessel sped.

In far America I found my God.
An Indian chief, Wachita, sought my aid
For dying Korsur of the Cheyenne tribe.
I followed him, still seeking human good;

The poisoned blood burned in old Korsur's veins,
But my true art prepared a healing balm.
Wonder awoke and Indian gratitude;
Four large white steers were yoked and offered me,
I took them not but asked that, in return,
The poor whom I might send may shelter there.
Old Korsur gazed intently and exclaimed
"Thou'rt Louis Bertrand, in a stranger form!
Those whom you send are welcome as my own."
Then searching in a bag of skin, he brought
A Roman Missal and "The Hermit's Prayer,"
And bade me keep them, saying that to him
They were no use, yet treasured for his sake
Who left them there—the missionary priest,
Great Louis Bertrand, the lone Indian's friend.
I took them and departed glad of heart.
All night I bent above the "Hermit's Prayer,"
Each word seemed fraught with peace unto my
        soul,
And when I finished, I had found the True.
In Faith, in Heaven, in Jesus Crucified—
Contrition wept o'er our confesional.
But peace was mine at last, deep peace of soul.
The rest you know. My soul had found the True.
"Resort to far Chartreuse" Al Rider said.
I too would kneel with that good hermit there
Who wrote "Duc, Domine, ad Te" and gaze—

                    Otho.

O Kaled, in that work I found my God!

                    Kaled.

And is't the same?

                    Otho.

            "Duc, Domine, ad Te!"
By name, "The Hermit's Prayer," I knew it not,
Nor knew that he who wrote it yet survived.

Kaled

True, name and history were, in my book,
Recorded by the pen of great Bertrand.
Read, Otho, ere the vesper bell shall chime,
"Duc, Domine, ad Te;" then let us pray:
Enough that round us are the eternal arms;
The storm may rave, we kneel secure in God.
Old Harp of Stelloburgum, sound once more
Fraught with the melody that saved our souls.

Otho.

My voice has not the depth of other days
But you shall hear "Duc, Domine, ad Te."

Duc, Domine, ad Te.

The soul was made for God, and unto Him
It must return therein to find its rest.
All evil is forgetfulness of God:
All sin rebellion 'gainst Omnipotence.
All things were made for man and man for God.
Man sets the creature on God's pedestal,
And offers homage to a kindred clay.

The years probationary hurry by,
Each day a mine, in whose exhaustless store,
Eternal treasures may be held secure.
The years replete with strivings heavenward,
With generous charity for all mankind,
With sacrifice of self and love of God,
Shall add new brilliance to the star set soul.
Time is the price of that eternity.
Here we must merit; past the pale of Death
Reward or punishment awaits the soul.
'Tis ours to serve and love our God on earth:
And is it hard to love Him? We do love
His attributes bound in the things of earth.
All beauty, all intelligence, all good.

78

All magnanimity, all wealth of soul,
All truth, all purity, all sanctity,
All worthy things of life—all—all of Good
Is a far gleaming from the All of God.
Man grasps this little good and calls it God.
Man seeks to satiate in finite joys
A soul created for infinity.
Were ocean's bed an empty void to-night,
And should we throw one cup of water there
'Twere still a burning, waste capacity.
Seek thou the soul's true end—union with God.

Unto that empty sea should one bird come,
Whose flight, thro' early morning, might collect
Some drops of rain; returning thus again
After one thousand years have passed away:
But when thro' countless ages, that lone bird
Shall have filled the broad Pacific whose proud
      waves
Shall rise storm-borne unto the dark'ning sky,
E'en then the soul shall live and, from its God,
Shall cry, "Eternity is just begun!
Truth, goodness, purity, and charity!
O never ending light, and love and life!
O knowledge, wisdom,—God-intelligence!
O beauty, symphony,—and this for aye!"
Deep praises roll from ransomed soul to soul
Caught by angelic waves and starry shores:
One grand Te Deum sounds from world to world.
E'en then the soul shall live, and from its pain,
Shall moan, "Eternity! eternity!"

Our crime is ignorance. We will not learn
The things of God. Kneel low, my child, with me;
Feel'st thou within thee immortality?
Then learn its origin, its destiny.

Almighty being is almighty love:
His rays divergent yet remain His own.

His rays distorted cease not to be His.
O'er rays distorted—erring human souls
The infinite Perfection gazed with love.
All earth was dark, it lay immersed in sin,
It knew not origin or destiny;
Its very life lay close embraced in death.
Almighty Love looked o'er a weary world:
A Babylon rejoiced, a Carthage mourned;
And souls were falling, as a long monsoon,
From bloody siege, from bloodier battle ground,
From funeral pyre, from Moloch's iron shrine.
Thro' all the avenues of Hell earth joined
Souls fell as drops that form the long monsoon:
And He whose goodness fills eternity,
Repented that His fiat had gone forth.
Annihilation were to strike Himself.
Love spoke in accents of the Trinity:
"'Tis ignorance of origin and end,
'Tis Lucifer's false glitter o'er the True,
'Tis yon barred Heaven. See in that fevered strife
Our own divinity in prison bonds,
In ignorance, in restlessness, in woe,
In aspiration to the unknown God.
I, clothed in human form, will go to earth
And teach the world its origin, its end"
He spoke; the angels trembled and adored
And veiled their faces in their snowy wings
To cry "all holy, holy, holy, Lord!"
Immensity awoke immensity.
Then slowly, mid the whiteness of the throne,
A burning cross—a Crucifix arose,
And God incarnate hung and suffered there.
Lo! cherubim and seraphim are dumb;
The Powers are still, and million angel choirs
And anthems of the voiceless waiting spheres
Are silent now. The mighty Crucified
From, "Consummatum est.' intoned the psalm
That broke the hushed concave from world to
        world.

Ring, cherubim and seraphim and powers
And principalities and angel choirs;
And ring, ye gates of Heaven re-opening,
And echo, blood-bought home bound human souls!

Behold the Crucifix, the book of Heaven
Who wills to read divinely, let him come
And kneel within my cave in wild Chartreuse,
Where all are welcome: and I promise peace.
O ye who drink at many a sullied fount,
O'er which the pure of heart read "Thirst again!"
Kneel low with me; and should the earthly damps
Obscure the light above yon Crucifix,
Return and pray.   I live to comfort thee
I live to lead the souls of God to God.

The last words blended with the vesper chime,
The desert silence and commune with God.

The morning rose; we sought the hermit's cave
"Pray for Al Rider, for our truest, lost!"

Kaled
Relate thy wanderings, Otho, thro' the past.

Otho.
Of little interest, and my rebel heart
Loses itself in great Al Rider's loss;
And gathering o'er me is a chill of soul.

Kaled.
Yet tell, where didst thou dwell these twenty years?

Otho.
I lingered long about Uraniberg,
Yet never entered more. As Autumn days
Grew weary o'er the world, I turned away.
A dream of Egypt's glory lingered still;

For, in a long forgotten childhood, lived
A fair haired mother whom I never knew;
A scene which memory conjures or retains
Of stern confusion; dark browed sullen men
With fierce red turbans over flashing eyes.
Hot angry words; "Mohammed! Christian! She
Will bring the curse of Allah on our homes!"
Quick flashed a scimetar,—low fell one form;
While strong hands siezed a crying child that
      turned
And bore impressed by fire this image hence.
A fair haired woman with both hands stretched
      forth,
Clasping her head whence issued streams of blood.
Her wild blue eyes fixed on me. Once I spoke
Of this to him who claimed to be my sire,
And his dark brow grew fearful. All that night
Fear dwelt with me; while, from his restless bed,
He raved of murder; then in gentler tone
He called "Natalia! Otho's fair haired bride,
Lone Alpine chamois! Matterhorn's gazelle!"
Then troubled he arose, but I had fled.

Towards Egypt I had turned, but Switzerland
Held my inconstant footsteps. Many a morn
From Alpine height I watched yon lordly orb
Break o'er the world thro' crimson belts of dawn.
'Twas evening. On the highest pinnacle
Accessible to foot of man I stood,
Watching a scene which might find place in
      Heaven.
Were our Al Rider here, he might portray
High silent arms of earth enclasped in heaven,
The bugle's call; the clear and far "good night!"
Long, long I lingered; dreaming of the True.
My brain grew dizzy,—pain abode with me,
I sought the downward path,—obscure it lay.
The bright blood gushed, a voice of song awoke,
And all things sang in darkness over me.

I felt, the first hour (in a waking dream),
That I had passed beyond the gates of Time,
And stood among the stars and heard their strain.
One choros rang across the universe,
Then faintly silenced in the galaxy.

Now earth encompassed me.—A dreary hut—
Wine, mystery, and lo! the opening door
Admits a woman weeping bitterly.
She heeds me not, I break the dreamy pause,
And speak of wondrous music lately stilled
"The monks below are chanting "Tenebrae."

With wide blue eyes, that look but see not, fixed;
And hands uplifted to her head she sang:

SONG.

Shall our weary forms repose
   In the Convent cemetery,
When the scene of life shall close
   O'er you and me?

Shall we lie together there,
   In the Convent cemetery?
No more parting, no more care
   For you and me.

Shall the peace prayer o'er us plead
   In the Convent cemetery;
And the white cross intercede
   For you and me?

Shall the sister-mounds arise
   In the Convent cemetery;
Angel pathways to the skies
   For you and me?

Or within the future gloom,
    Do our union ways diverge?
Shall the space-winds o'er each tomb
    Moan a dirge?

O God grant that we repose
    In the Convent cemetery!
When the scene of life shall close
    O'er you and me.

The while I seemed to see the Egyptian home,
The fair-haired woman with both hands upreared
Clasping her head, whence issued streams of blood.

The song was ended, and the hands drooped low.
The woman slept or lived in phantasy.

Revived; with morning glory I arose
And sought to hasten from the strange abode,
Yet fascinated, turned. The woman rose
And pressed upon me hospitality.
A gracefulness, a dignity, a spell—
A high mysterious sorrow—while my mind
Repeated from the dark man's wanderings,
"Lone Alpine chamois, Otho's fair-haired bride!—"

Kaled, we would not drag our minds to-day
Thro' graves of evil. Thoughts contaminate,
And he who waits us in the hermit's cave
Would have our souls as Jungfrau's sky-borne
        snows.
That woman was my mother. Twenty years
I held the hand of duty as the True.—
Lo! Bruno's grave—beyond the Hermit dwells.

Kaled.

Of all that comes to us we but receive
The measure of our capacity.   Kneel down
Here let us cleanse our souls in contrite prayer.

Otho.

Thou art the worthier, Kaled, yet I feel
That I shall see yon Truth unveiled to-day.
A hand of ice is grasping my old heart
Can this be death?—

Kaled.

Haste to the hermit's cave.
My Otho, is it thus the drama ends?
Yet linger, for we stand within the cave;
The Hermit yonder prostrate as in prayer.
One cry from Otho, joyous, anguished, last—
We gazed, we saw—our own Al Rider—dead.

HELEN.

It was a London hospital conducted by Sisters. Helen, the night nurse, had just completed the well worn round. She had held the cup to the fevered lip, her cool fingers had soothed the burning brow, her kind heart had left its benison on all—even the sleepers.

It was the last night of the old year. Helen stood by her window watching the myriad lights of the city; smiling as the meaningless jangling of bells, shouts, and cannon roars arose from the distant throng. What power was there in the spirit óf the place, the hour, to annihilate thirty years,—so that Helen, the night nurse of fifty, was Helen, the actress of twenty? What rich veins of sentiment and sorrow lie in the rugged, every day hearts by which we are surrounded! Each life is a battery of broken circuit. Deep in the soul lies the potent cell; thence issuing they lie—the negative pole in the logical sense, the positive pole in the heart's affections. In passive potency they lie until God's hands shall have rested in benison on both; then shall the joyous currents run throughout the ages of ages.

The night nurse stood in revery. Not weak, not even tender was the heart. The London skies grew Arctic still and pure and cold; the London towers grew iceberg shadows o'er pure snows; the London lights grew faint Aurora amber. In the dream light came the children, happy school girls with yellow hair, who pelted one another with Dandelion balls. But amid the group the merriest eyes of all gazed earnestly on the dreamer. The night nurse murmured mournfully, "O Childhood! do you not know me?"

With the dream light mingled love-light. Far away on life's horizon, wondrous blue eyes, gem-like, star-like, God-like rose in zenith splendor to the Northern Constellations, mid the stars which rise and set not. That star was shining to-night and in its distance Pain moaned in the arms of the cirrus cloud; and in its smile Forgiveness tinged the world and waiting skies; and in its tenderness the crimson streamers trembled down the dawn, the wondrous Aurora rose o'er the world and the heart of the dreamer grew weak,—yes weak and tender.

With the love light mingled death light. A mother's face slept as a lily 'mid lilies—slept and awoke not; a mother's hands held the frost blossom in peace and extended not, welcomed not; a mother's heart lay cold at last, while upon the waiting face, about her as an atmosphere lingered the longing, the waiting, the love that had killed her. Kiss her again, not with the old passionate anguish, but with a tender sorrow, the child of the life years.

Unusual sounds ascending from the city ended the wanderings of memory. A fire had burst forth apparently on the Strand. Madly the flames leaped up to the darkening sky. Helen prayed long and earnestly; prayed for those who might even now be suffering in the flames, prayed for the dark tide of humanity shouting, struggling toward the scene of disaster; prayed for those dear to her whether they wander in Time or wait in eternity, prayed for the world.

HARP ECHOES.

"Dying and calling for you!" O Mother, blest star
    of my childhood!
Sink not yet in the western world till thy prodigal
    finds thee;
Place thy dear hand on my head, and murmur the
    words of forgiveness.

Time stands still, and the distance between us
increases.
Train, and vessel of steam, ye are painted forms
and ye move not.
Oh! for the speed of desire, and I tread you to-
night, native city,
On, on, on, from the pier, to the home, to the heart
of my mother.
Has she grown haggard and wan? O God! I recall
the last parting;
Heart broken, passionate prayer that I pause for
the love that is pleading
Pause on the threshold of error, and turn to the
loves of my childhood;
Pause—but the pleading voice was hushed in the
smile of a lover;
While thro' my mother's tears, I saw the glittering
foot-lights,
The curtain about to rise, the crowd, the low waiting of music,
And, tearing away from her arms I left her prostrate in anguish.
"Dying, and calling for you." Ye sentinel stars
o'er the city!
Bless all the world as it sleeps, and cherish the children of London.
Pain is the guest of my soul. I stand by the dark
peaceful waters
Where they have sought long repose,—the children
of error and sorrow.
Sisters, who stood where I stand, who sought what
the dark waters promise,
I, too, long for its peace, and scarcely my sorrow
condemns you.
May ye have found rest at last, ye wretched, ye
strong ones!
Life is a wearisome way, but surely some eye is
above us

That watches from cause to close, and pities the
  sorrows of mortals.
Dawn by the eastern sky. Farewell, Fred Ashton,
  my husband,
Sadie and Wilson and Nell.—'Tis the train that
  conveys to the steamer.
How will it be in the western world; and what of the
  future!

PART SECOND.

Nearer that central thing, that coffin upborne by
  the lilies;
Delicate Russian frost-flowers that spring from the
  heart of the sleeper.
Heart that I made thus cold; but I, too, am dying,
  my mother!
Dying to lie as you lie, and never to waken or
  sorrow.
When will it come,—the end of this insupportable
  anguish?
Mother, O Mother! yet rest. I know all and I must
  endure it;
Late, too late have I come, and yet I must live and
  endure it.
If he comes in—the man who stabbed ere I stabbed
  the dead woman,
What shall we murderers say?—She called him
  husband, I—father.
Yet could the proud lips move, they would seal yet
  deeper the silence
That hangs over fatherless years, and meaningless,
  sad lamentations.
Better to go as I came, and, o'er the mysterious
  ocean,

Join in the throngs of men,—a sigh in a sob
    universal,
Asking the whence and the whither, the why, and
    the wherefore of living.
Cease, this pain at my heart! Something is draw-
    ing my life blood.
How does she look in the face? I have groaned at
    her feet in the lilies.
Take them from face and hands—those cloths—and
    the weights from the eye-lids.
Bend o'er the dear dead face, and gather it close
    to my bosom;
Will not the agony there awaken its slumbering
    sister?
Wake, for the answer is here; oh! waken thou
    carvéd Expectance!
Go not thus to the grave, thou Question forever
    unanswered!
Lo! I have come—had I known—Sink fond head
    on the pillow;
Haunt me forevermore, thou Waiting embodied in
    marble;
Live in the world, in the sea, in the sky, till I
    cease, till I die.

II.

Out from the dead and away, mid the gathering
    lights of the city.
Phantoms and falling snows, and I hurry, one mid
    the many.
Ten years passed in a night, and youth has forever
    departed.
Yet could I weep for the throng, some indefinable
    sorrow
Passes from me to them and rests upon me and the
    human.
Forever   hurrying   onward,   phantasmagorical
    changes,

Perhaps she will pass this way; the lights and the
feathery stillness
Were not unmeet for her feet. I smell the odor
of lilies,
All things cease to revolve, and the world is
petrified Waiting.

III.

Out on the ocean again, silent, yet inwardly
sobbing
As a fresh grief must be—ever ready to lash at
the heart strings.
Heavily falling snows, sequester the vanishing
city:
Mourn o'er the form in the hearse and the long
black funeral procession.
Peace o'er the waiting grave kissed by the whisper-
ing spirits;
Mourned by the frozen tears that fall from my soul
o'er the city.
Mother, my mother, good-by! Good-by, thou
noblest of women!
Roll away carriages, roll, and echo the hoofs of the
horses;
One of the many is sleeping in peace from the
surges of sorrow,
And she will not waken.

O thou mysterious ocean!
Have you some anguish of soul, some mighty o'er-
mastering sorrow;
That you thus moan and lament and murmur a
long incompleteness?
Last of the Western world—the Goddess of Liberty
blesses:

Sea birds are singing "forgiveness," and sea gulls
    are murmuring "duty."
Long, long, long, have I died with the dead, but I
    live with the living.

IV.

To-morrow we land in England. How still is the
    bosom of ocean!
Over the home of the cirrus-cloud and under the
    earth borne waters,
Wanders the Regent of night sedate mid her glitter-
    ing companions.
Thus she was lying, poor heart! mid the restless
    life of the city,
Just one week from to-night, and I crushed her
    shroud and her lilies,
And fell, like a wounded thing, to the street from
    the balcony gate-way;
Leaving the great door locked and the dead with
    another sad secret.
How is it now, O my Mother! Moonlight and
    star-light o'er Greenwood
Glide among spectral tombs and straggling shad-
    ows of pine trees,
Glide over snow laden spruce trees and low winding
    covers of myrtle;
Over the paupers' square and monuments lordly
    of rich men;
Over the little grave of the brother who wailed
    for an hour
E'en at the portals of Life—and over the new grave
    beside him.
Moonlight and starlight and shadows, join in a
    Requiem o'er them;
Sighs o'er the graves, combine and wail on the
    midnight their dirge;
Winds of the sullen dawn, murmur their last
    lamentation.

V.

Why do I stand in England? A sob from a sorrow
 subsiding
Answers in meaning vague, and consonant with
 other feelings.
Shall I go back to the stage and join Fred Ashton,
 my husband?
Fred with his winning face and character weak and
 ignoble;
Wanting in self-command, and the power to will
 and to will not;
Fred with his fortified word strongly defended by
 promise,
Fred in the ruins by night, o'ercome by a breath of
 temptation:
Fred with his happy blue eyes and girl-like beauty
 of person:
Made by God to be loved as she loves him,—the
 desolate mother
Who follows his erring way and worships the sin
 in the sinner.
Yet I recall the night when life was bitterly
 earnest;
Fear and deep pain were mine, and death stood
 waiting a victim.
All my soul cried for him then, and the woman-
 heart weak as a child-heart
Suddenly, sternly died in the call and the answer
 that came not.
Yet o'er the hurried past whose sobbings yet break
 from the ocean,
Joining the chiming of bells and far American
 lilies,
Surging from public applause to an infant wail into
 silence,
Touching all things of life, from childhood to
 dreams that are passing—
Wide and warm as the sunset sky lies the buried
 affection.

PART THIRD

Calling me back to life again when I thought to
  have laid down
All broken links of a chain that never can be
  re-united.
Yet fair is the new world with flowers and loves of
  the beautiful spring time!
Sweet is the first smile of life after pain and the
  long shore of shadows!
Ten long months have I wrestled with pain and the
  pitiless fever;
And they have nursed me well—those gentle voiced
  Sisters of Mercy.
Pictures upon the walls, ye speak of peace and a
  haven
Where there is peace of soul. There bends St.
  Louis Gonzaga.
Why is that face so grand bending over the skull
  and the crucifix?
Half would I know whence its peace and the depth
  of that mystic Religion
Whose strong, pure children look out from the ages
  upon me.
St. Bruno in hoary Chartreuse, the harp of the
  martyred Cecelia;
The boy Pancratius in prayer waiting death in the
  Roman arena;
Grand Augustine clasping a peace o'er the cold
  human altar;
The Mother of Sorrows looks down, the Wander-
  ing Sheep and the Shepherd.
Beautiful faces of saints, ye are poems in language
  of angels;

Speak yet again to my soul, and I earnestly seek
    that Religion
Which made you strong to endure and noble in
    combat.
Oh! may it be for me, that, after the drama of
    error,
I may yet act in real life a part that is noble?
May there be peace for my soul in this Roman
    Religion?
She in the grave loved it not, and I would embark
    for her heaven—
Heaven—and Hell—and the soul—some Sunday
    School murmurs from childhood
Break thro' the long dark years. O Pater,
    peccavi!
Lips of the strong saints move, and utter one long
    miserere!
Lo! from the ruins! God, lo, from the ruins!
Lo! I will paint my sin, the sin and its hasty
    requital.
Black was the back-ground, my God, yea, sullen
    and wild were the heavens
Bright was the flame, O my soul! as it leaped on
    wings to the starless;
Aye, tragic and grand was the scene, but I marked
    not the palace consuming.
Black is the back-ground, my God, but blacker the
    desolate ruins;
Ceased is the treacherous flame, but ceaseless the
    moan of the night wind.
Lo from the ruins! God! lo, from the ruins!
Angel of pity, forbear, nor answer contrition with
    justice!
God of the erring, enfold my sin in the mantle of
    mercy.

CONCLUSION.

Fire in the London Theatre! How madly those
    flames lash the darkness!
Horrible sounds fill the air; lo, the bells tell the
    death of the old year.
God—that great building in flames! Say not it is
    crowded with mortals.
Hope, yet hope—they are out; for escapes there
    are many.
Well do I know every board of the Strand Covent
    Garden.
Strange to recall, thirty years from this night that
    I stood there
With Sadie and Wilson and Nell and Fred Ashton,
    my husband;
Thirty years from this night came the news that my
    mother
Was dying and calling for me. O Destiny, guard-
    ian of mortals!
Lead you to Heaven at last? I have trodden cir-
    cuitous mazes,
Nor would I re-live one day of the life that is
    passing.
Old am I now, and my heart is cold without pain or
    affection;
Yet in their time pressed graves, they shudder—
    dead pleasures and sorrows.
O how slowly they died! How long in life's deso-
    late chambers,
Gaunt white ghosts they repined; but they spoke
    not, they hoped not;
Only gazed out on the past, and knew not they
    shaded the future.

So lies our dying babe, unknowing he causes the
  anguish
That breaks o'er the still, white face of the desolate mother;
Kisses and prayers and tears, but the soul is
  departing.
Yes, ye died hard and long—life's mighty
  affections!

II.

Lower, yet lower, the flame; but long has my old
  heart been dreaming.
Born is the bright New Year, like a willing king
  o'er a kingdom
That clasps the unknown to unknown, and smiles
  at the sad face departing.
Yet is our God over all, the thirty years I have
  passed here;
Caring for dying and dead, and assuaging life
  sorrows;
Doing for God's dear sake the work of a Sister of
  Mercy—
Never aspiring to them but having their God, their
  Religion,
These years look on me to-day, and their faces are
  peaceful.
Yet would I know of the answer to prayer. In the
  waiting hereafter,
All must be well with those I have loved; for is it
  not written
"Ask and you shall receive!" Heart and life have
  been asking
Heaven for those souls I have loved; Heaven to
  each devious pathway,
Pathways that rise from the grave, and pathways
  that wind amid error.

"Ask and ye shall receive." To the God of the dead
    and the living—
Merciful Father of all! heart and life have been
    asking—
"And ye shall receive!"

III.

Long has the night-nurse slept. List! the vesper
    bell of the New Year.
There is slow pain at my heart,—a sob from a
    slumbering sorrow.
Ah! I was dreaming last night, but here is the
    present and duty;
Patience and prayer lead away to the beds of the
    sick and the dying.

IV.

He will not need my care, 'round whom priest and
    sisters are kneeling,
Bearing our great, good God to the soul on its
    terrible journey.
"O Christian soul, depart to thy Judge and thy
    Saviour!"
Still, all still,—move away, leave the nurse with the
    dead man.
"Burned in the London theatre!" I gaze for the
    first time
On the still face of the dead. I have pressed down
    the eyelids
Ere my dim eyes discern that the dead is Fred
    Ashton, my husband.
Cry not, O heart, in thy pain; we have learned to
    endure and to suffer!
Press it down, let it moan, let it writhe, let it
    conquer!

Life for one word! O bend low, hold his head on
    my bosom;
Back to his old love at last! Kiss his brow, kiss
    his eyelids!—
Break for his soul from the frozen pain the long
    De Profundis:
Gratitude, bring me my tears; he has died with the
    rites of Religion.
Old heart, God watches o'er all. Rise, be strong
    and be silent.
Now is the corpse in the dead-room alone, and the
    night-nurse—on duty.

BERNARDUS.

Imperious winds of winter stir the trees,
My stately forest bends at their weak call
Obeying Him who speaks beyond the voice.
O Life, that wanders hand in hand with Death!
Commutual agents of a common cause!
Thy mysteries gather round me, but I bow
Obeying Him who speaks beyond the voice.

Loved solitude, loved pain! Can I be he
Who, glowing in the light of noble lives,
Arose and cried for combat, cried for souls?
Cried strongly; for o'er borne on ocean winds,
Saddening the skies of golden Italy,
Came wailings from the far America
That souls were dying, grand Italian souls
Rich with the breath of nobles of the world.
Then came the torch that burned all human ties.
"Bernardus," ran the letter from Pauline,
"Vittorio is dead: alas for me!
They killed him, Father, killed Vittorio.
With morning he went laughing from my side.
(You know the soul of truth, the heart of fire.)
'Tis midnight. Lo! he sleeps and shall not rise.
O burning heart, thy first rest and thy last!
O soul of fire, to be so cold, so low!
They killed him, but his death knell waits for mine."

Pauline, fair child, Vittorio the true,
And is it thus the bright America
Unrolls the silver scroll that star-like shone?
In yonder Abbey's shade I see you now

Chasing your golden childhood. Now I stand
Before the white procession scaling thee
True heart—to heart so sadly falsely true.
And now—O scene unknown! Too late I go
From thee, Italian skies, Italian home;
To late I come to thee, white land of souls.

Ah me! from this low bed I live once more
One year, whose every moment was a love
Immersed in God, diffused o'er human souls.
I fought, I conquered; and a prostrate self
Lamenting, freed its caged divinity
Which bounding to its center, walked with God,
Thence God-like walked with men. Then kindred
        souls
Responsive rose, and rich the harvest grew
Of souls for God. From far Loretto's pines
To fair Los Angeles, the fields were mine.
Oh! how I felt the God within me speak,
As, Sunday mornings, 'neath the lordly pines,
I rose to bless my cherished country-men:
I rose to plead the cause of Heaven with them,
To gild the mystery o'er human lives;
To open yon eternity and show
The perfect thing,—the broken chrysalis.
In the dark depths of restless longing eyes,
A peace arose, a reverent content:
While an electric circle thro' that throng
Bore love to me and passed with love to them.

Perhaps, grown God-like in commune with God,
Uprising Self had seen the adoring throng,
And my strong intellect, with poison-pride
Of Lucifer, had said, "Non serviam."
It may have been so. God ordains the best,
And this I know,—that yon eternity
Is calling me, and I approach nor fear.
The end of life secured, calmly we view

Those guideless rests and wanderings on the way,
Those hours replete with fate, those joys and griefs,
And that great combat where the soul has bled.

Aye, calmly now I hear the Oregon,
Bewailing to the pines the gathering storm.
Great trees that stood unmoved yet moaned because
My thousands waited me beneath the storm.
I hear the rain, the thousand liquid balls
Break on the trees that hid the scowling skies.
I feel again the apprehensive chill
As like strong demons, from a battle ground
Precipitate, yet closed in burning strife,
The lightnings struggled mid the crashing trees.
Why, as encircled thus I looked to Heaven,
Did falling trees and thunder from the flash
Sound mid the flame, "Bernardus, God is kind!"
This had the demon heard? that, from the strife,
Perceived me, recognized a soul to know
In that bright world his birth-right forfeit throne;
And crashing thus in mocking maddened power,
Assails me, strikes me, permeates my blood—
A poison-fire; and my strong sinews bind
In fixed contortions; while the glorious eyes
Close in his light forever. Now I feel
The death hand crushing, too unkind to kill.
Ah well! calm evening came, but I had grown
Blind Old Bernardus. O the fierce Cannae!
While my hot spirit loathed the hideous bonds,
And latent pride cried long, "Non serviam!"
And all the hopes of all the years wailed loud.
While, rushing from the future, grim despairs
Assailed the white robed Peace which weeping said,
"His will be done. Bernardus, God is kind."

But as the peace-prayer sank in human cries,
And the white tears grew blood upon the plain;
Faith stretched across the sky a wondrous bow

That rising eastward, touched the western shore;—
A scarlet band of beauty; thereon traced
As it were of snowy mist and foamy wings
The words, "Eternity! Eternity!"
By day, by night, it shone above the strife;
Divinely kind, a weeping sympathy.
Grand o'er my night of day, my night of night.
While I beheld a thousand silent things
Rise from the earth unto the crimson skies.
There as a mighty vortex summoned them,
All came, all sank in that "Eternity."
And now the sky is dark, horizon bound,
With restless things that ever more ascend,
And ever more approach and fall therein.
My conquered spirit cried, "this scene must be
The things of Time which meet eternity."
Ah! life of pain that soon shall cry no more,
Eternal spirit soon to wander free,
Endure thy strange companionship awhile
And breathe, with that dim echo 'round the world,
"His will be done. Bernardus, God is kind."

SONGS OF HOME AND SONGS OF HEAVEN.

There are plenty to extol the hero of the battle-field, to sing the sorrows and delights of love, to lament over the sorrows of the living, over the graves of the dead; but oh! for an angel voice, sounding from shore to shore, to sing the song of Heaven. Sounding o'er the narrow alley, the wretched court where children live and know not they are wretched. Sounding in the lone attic, the damp basement where all day long, all night long moan poverty, neglect, disease. Sounding where lie irrevocable wrong, misunderstanding, change, grief, which only the grave can heal.

Surely it is our grandest theme. By whatsoever name it may be called—Nirvana, Valhalla, Elysium, Heaven, we mean the abode of peace, of never ending happiness which the human heart craves, which reason demands, which Religion promises. Say as our wisest have said that there are differences which we cannot reconcile, mysteries which we cannot understand; but say more earnestly in union with the innate voice of the soul, with the noblest aspirations of earth's noblest children,—that Good is paramount; that Love is the name of that almighty Being so silently guiding universes; that evil shall, in the Divine economy, conduce to good; that death is the liberation of the soul. One voice has spoken over the gloom of the grave, and the sorrow which hears that voice becomes a holy joy: "I am the Resurrection and the Life; he who believeth in me, although he were dead, shall live; and every one who liveth and believeth in me shall not meet with eternal death." What joy these words have brought to earth! It is worth being a Christian just to repeat them to the sorrowing heart, to murmur them low and solemnly amid the lamentation of the soul when we kneel by our dead. Behold the mother bending over the white death-sleep of her child, whose every feature becomes more beautiful, more intensely dear while she gazes; whose words and actions rise like great flood waves over her soul while she gazes! Whose words shall console that brokenness of heart? His who made that heart; "I am the Resurrection and the Life." Like the white cloud mist of the morning shall fall Religion's requiem; like the steady radiance of Rigel in the winter sky shall shine Religion's promises.

We see the child standing by the still form of a father, bending over the ashy cheek, the thin, white hair, the lifeless clasp of the cold hands. Who shall take from her the faith in the prayer which nature teaches her to pour forth; the prayer for the welfare of that dear soul; the prayer that they shall meet again in a better world? The hand that would stretch out over the darkness of human life, and drag down that light shining from Heaven, is the hand of a demon.

We stand beside the woman who has sinned and suffered. We remember the meek Christ who said, "Neither do I condemn thee." Words of kindness are spoken, words of hope.

We stand by the infirm old man tottering to the long rest of the grave. Words of kindness are spoken, words of hope.

We stand by those long monotonous lives which daily take up their burdens simply and earnestly, not knowing that they are heroes. Words of kindness are spoken, words of hope because we believe in the promises of Christ.

Shine, star of earth, the hope that points to Heaven!
Calm o'er each life let thy soft splendor fall;
What else shall heal the world-wound hourly given?
What else shall answer when the erring call?

What else shall gild the gloom above the grave?
What else shall solace where the heart has bled?
What else shall shine with power o'er land and
    wave,
And promise us again our dead, our dead?

Shine o'er the night, the night of strife and wrong;
Shine where e'er sorrow sits, and evil sleeps;
Shine o'er the awakening of a weary world;
Shine where Religion weeps.

THE LARGE-PRINT BIBLE.

The large-print Bible is open wide
    On my mother's knee;
But her head is back, and the closed eyes see
The children that once played 'round her knee,
    And the merry look,
    From the apron nook,
And the clasp that lies on the finger-stained book.

The large-print Bible is open wide
On my mother's knee; but the still tears glide
    Through the sheltering hand;
The silence is hard to understand.
And her dreams call aloud, call aloud
To the pitiful pride of the proud,

To the wanderers that walk with the crowd.
To the bright eyes that sleep in a shroud.
    Call aloud, call aloud
To the pattering rain
That breaks on the plain,
That it come back again
    To the cloud!

The large-print Bible is open wide
On my mother's knee, but grief is still,
    For she lies in a golden dream:
And I kiss the brow and the thin gray hair
And the tear from the cheek and the wet eye lash,
And I hold her close till the children come
And laugh in the sun-light of childhood home,
Then pass thro' a cloud world angel bright
    Into twilight and night.
But they sing as they fade in the air
"Of that home of the soul bright and fair,"
And the welcome awaiting her there.
    "In the sweet by and by"
We shall meet, we shall part never more:
    Hush the sob, hush the sigh,
    In the old lullaby
Of the babes on the beautiful shore.

    "In the sweet by and by"
Where the pain and the parting are o'er,
Where the wanderer shall wander no more,
Where the love world shall love as of yore.
"We shall meet on that beautiful shore."

THE ANGELUS.

Day was weaving shreds with twilight:
Sank the sun into the West.
Lingering rays blushed over ocean
And the scene held magic rest.

Came the echoes from the city
(Faintly sank into the sea.)
Of the bells, the minstrel keepers
Of the time years' treasury.

Far the Angelus was ringing,
And we knelt together there;
While the sun's last ray departed,
And the sea moaned thro' our prayer.

I have stood by other oceans
Traversed many a weary shore,
But the fullest glow of beauty
There departing, rose no more.

Far the Angelus is ringing,
Faintly stealing o'er the sea;
And a star of memory shineth
In the great eternity.

CREDO.

That all of evil shall be good
That, bending to the earthy plain,
Some hand shall pluck the Tree of Ill
And all its lingering roots of pain,
                    Hoc credo.

That want of knowledge is not sin,
Nor is its blighting progeny;
That crime is never what it seems,
But what it is on Calvary,
                    Hoc credo.

That God shall call across the world,
And Time shall answer from its birth.
That, in a realm where death is not,
My soul shall meet the loves of earth,
                    Hoc credo.

THOUGHTS.

They tell me I shall die. There looms a night
Whose sequent dawning I shall never see;
Or there shall be a dawn whose sequent night,
Benignly coming, cometh not to me.

A little ceremony, a few tears;
A requiem pleading for the parted soul;
A little wonder from the passing crowd
That sighs as onward the dark hearse shall roll;

And I shall sleep low with the mighty dead,
And I shall know all that the dead now know:
Shall be as uncommunicative too
Concerning certain rites we undergo.

Above me shall the fruitful seasons roll,
Above me shall the storms of Winter rave,
Shall Summer thro' the breeze borne boughs
        complain
And bend in light and shadow o'er my grave.

Such is earth earthy, and we fear it not
If homeward bound the glorious soul shall soar;
Nor cease to live within the smile of God,
Nor cease to exult from star-bound shore to shore:

Nor cease to exult for all eternity.
Oblivious of the narrow things of earth;
All conscious of the glorious destiny
Vibrating in the strong eternal birth.

EASTER BELLS.

Loud the Easter bells are ringing,
Alleluias fill the air;
"Resurrexit, sicut dixit!"
Bend, O grateful world! in prayer.

Echoes rise from cliff and wildwood,
All the world is glad;
I recall the home of childhood,
And my heart is sad.

Ring God's promise o'er the wide world,
Linger o'er my home;
Tell the loving hearts that wait there
Of that world to come.

Say that dark ways shall be made plain,
Say that loved ones never roam;
Ring, O bells, across the wide world,
Linger o'er my home.

RENUNCIATION.

What I gave away for God
That I keep for Heaven;
I have furrowed deep the sod,
And my dear one given.
Ne'er on earth to clasp thy hand,
Meet in the better land.

Meet me where the farewell song
Never wakes a sigh;
Meet me where the clouds of wrong
Never dim the sky.
Ne'er on earth to clasp thy hand
Meet me in the better land.

Meet me where our souls are pure
As yon lamps of even;
Meet me where our loves endure
As the loves of Heaven.
Ne'er on earth to clasp thy hand
Meet me in the better land.

JUST BECAUSE ONE BABY DIED.

Who shall pause or who shall listen
Mid the moving tide?
Who shall know how hearts can suffer
Just because one baby died?

Who shall know that all life's sorrow
Knelt by baby's bed and cried,
While pain chilled the golden ringlets
And she died?

Who shall know that all earth withered
Unto compass, coffin-wide;
Unto one still form with lilies,
Just because one baby died?

Where the myrtle ivy slumber
Even now a tear is dried,
And I love the whole world better,
Just because one baby died.

Other faces now surround me,
Other footsteps bid me guide;
Life is kinder, Heaven is nearer
Just because one baby died.

HEAVEN.

Earth-children, there is rest in Heaven:
Strong choirs shall raise the psalm sublime
That lulls all strife in victory,
While Toil shall sob far down in Time.

Earth-children, there is joy in Heaven:
For standing where the Sinless stood
All malice falls from each desire,
And all that pleases,—must be good.

Earth-children, there is love in Heaven:
The idol shrined within each breast
Shall live, shall love its devotee,
Our saddest here is Heaven's best.

Earth-children, there is peace in Heaven:
And we shall sorrow never more;
The time-storm's circling billows roll
In gentlest surges on that shore.

Earth-children, thus the dreamer dreams,
And thus the prayer for you ascends.
My heart is kind for all the world,
And all the world and I are friends.

THE ANGEL.

I bend o'er the dead in the white robed bed
While the farewell sighs are given,
I breathe on the air from the censer of prayer
That the home of the soul is Heaven.

I bend o'er the world with my banner unfurled
Till the night of sorrow is gone,
I murmur of peace where the soul surges cease,
And the ages of Heaven roll on.

My throne is Faith, my palace is Death;
And I am a Voice that is given
To cry sublime, o'er the sorrows of time,
That the home of the soul is Heaven.

EUGENE.

Just a beauteous baby sleeping.
Smiling to the angels' call;
And a mother vigil keeping
Dreaming—that was all.

Just a part of fate unfolding
Silent as a falling star,
Guiding baby through the waters
To the "Gates ajar."

Just a little life-way ending
Where the purest lilies blow:
Straight, unstained, amid the mazes
Lost in crime and woe.

Silent watchers vigil keeping;
Earth bound while the angels call,
And a lonely mother weeping,
Praying—that was all.

EUGENE.

O hearts that mourn above the dead!
Yet hear an angel strain:—
"All silent is the waiting bed,
But ye shall rise again."

"Since Jesus wept above the dead.
Thy sorrow may complain;
He whispers low whose heart has bled,—
The dead shall rise again."

"While Faith is pleading o'er thy dead,
Oh! murmur thro' thy pain,—
All silent is the waiting bed,
But we shall rise again."

HOMES THAT ARE DESOLATE.

Homes that are desolate! Ah! my mother sits
Artist divine, within the lonely room,
While wondrous visions rise 'neath her deep **tender**
    eyes,
And forms that are not walk in memory gloom.
      For on the vacant air
      There are faces wondrous fair,
      There are youthful footsteps springing,
      There is guileless laughter ringing,
      There are childish voices singing,
      Scene of light, angel bright!
There is love its vigil keeping,
O'er the couch of beauty sleeping:
Silence deep, rosy sleep,
        Holy night!

For, on the vacant air,
There are faces filled with care;
And the voices die away
In a melancholy lay,
    And a groan;
For a pale child bows the head,
And upon the breast lies dead.
    Loved Leone!
Weary winds of Winter rave
While we lay her in the grave,
Silent snows breathe repose
While the north wind wildly blows.

For a brave heart touched the shadow
Where Life's promises begin:
    There was sin.
    Ah—well!
Then his country called away,
And he donned the sombre Gray,
    And he fell.

They are coming from the child-world,
From the love world, from the home,
From the sorrow, from the battle,—
To the dreamer, lo! they come.

AMAMUS TE.

For the heart that heard earth moan
Thro' the strain the spheres intone,
Sought the soul and quit the throne;
                    Amamus Te.

For the soul in agony
Keeping its sublime decree
In the stern Gethsemani;
                    Amamus Te.

For the weary pathway pressed,
For the Cross and thorny rest,
Unto "Consummatum est;"
                    Amamus Te.

PRAYER.

Stay beneath me in the valley,
All of earthly care,
While my spirit seeks the mountain
Pinnacled in prayer.

O my soul's love Heart of Jesus!
While the earth clouds roll,
Raise me to Thee, great Ideal,
Inundate my soul.

In thy high transcendent beauty,
Let my spirit lie
As Arcturus now reposes
In the midnight sky.

Take from me, all that offends Thee,
Make my life like thine;
Patient, noble, generous, god-like—
Human life divine.

Cleanse my soul in anguished burning,
Fires of Purity!
Teach the majesty of sorrow,
Lone Gethsemane!

Lead me down into the valley;
I will meet life's part:
Strengthened in the holy love light
Of the Sacred Heart.

REST.

Our hearts can find no place of rest
Until they seek that fount above,
Deep in the City of the Blest
Where all love joins eternal Love.

Thou art, O God! my soul's repose.
And if I never rest in Thee
I am forever as the bird
That wings a world beneath the sea.

My soul is portion of Thy soul:
As Thou art, so am I—divine
And if I join Thee not again,
Eternal isolation mine.

STORM.

Thou art the sea-gull resting on the wave,
    O prayerful human soul!
The storm is on the deep, the lightning blast,
Upborne by echoing thunders, cuts the vast,
    And Ural ranges roll:
Black skies descending sink into the wave,—
    O bird! O human soul!
Above, within, encompassed, and alone,
Deep in the death world, and not doomed to die.
    Bright star of our goal,
While we wait o'er our deathless graves
    Shine strong in Eternity's sky!

RESURREXIT.

He is risen, we shall rise!
Bid the paean roll,
Thrilling to the zenith skies,
From each ransomed soul.

Sing it o'er the sobbing waves
Bathed in sunset glow;
Sing it o'er the waiting graves
Robed in purest snow.

Sunset banners are unfurled,
And my soul is still:
Clasping hands beyond the world,
Willing but Thy will.

RETURN.

Jesus watching on our altar,
To Thy patient love we come:
We are weary, we have wandered
Far, oh! far from home.

Faith is singing songs of childhood,
Old emotions fill the breast;
Low the Altar-voice is sighing
"Come to me and rest."

FAITH.

Credo that Jesus died for me,
That I shall live eternally,
   In pleasure or in pain;
That since His eucharistic birth,
The Son of God remains on earth,
   And ever shall remain.

That o'er the world, from end to end,
The eyes of a kind Father bend
   In pity o'er His own:
That every heartfelt prayer is heard,
Contrition's sigh and trembling word,
   And Sorrow's meekest moan:

That laying down the earth worn heart,
And rising from its mortal part,
   My spirit shall be free;
Ethereal bound across the night,
To be a beauty truth and light
   For all eternity.

PEACE.

Across the night, with silent pinions furled
The angels sang a song of peace
   Unto a sleeping world.
O'er the guardian lights of cities,
O'er the winding river's bed,
O'er the forests, o'er the fountains,
   This is what they said:

"Sister world, we know thy sorrow,
But we know thy wondrous home:
Rise to-night, and rest to-morrow
Never more to roam.

Sister world, thy unveiled darkness
Is supernal light:
Truth is paramount and Reason
And eternal Right."